About the Author

Bernard Ashley is one of the most highly regarded authors in this country. Born in Woolwich, south London, he was evacuated during the war, and ended up attending fourteen different primary schools. After school, Bernard did National Service in the RAF where he 'flew' a typewriter. He then went on to become a teacher and later a headteacher – his two most recent posts being in east and south London, areas which have provided him with the settings for many of his books. Bernard now writes full time.

Bernard Ashley's other novels for the Black Apple list include *Tiger Without Teeth*, a *Guardian* Book of the Week, *Little Soldier*, which was shortlisted for the *Guardian* Children's Book Award and the Carnegie Medal and *Revenge House*.

'Bernard Ashley's greatest gift is to turn what seems to be low-key realism into something much stronger and more resonant.' *Philip Pullman*

ALSO BY BERNARD ASHLEY

LITTLE SOLDIER

Shortlisted for the Carnegie Medal and the Guardian Children's Book Award

TIGER WITHOUT TEETH

REVENGE HOUSE

ORCHARD BOOKS
96 Leonard Street, London EC2A 4XD
Orchard Books Australia
32/45-51 Huntley Street, Alexandria, NSW 2015
ISBN 1 84121 306 3
First published in Great Britain in 2003
A paperback original
Text © Bernard Ashley 2003
The right of Bernard Ashley to be identified as the author
of this work has been asserted by him in accordance with
the Copyright, Designs and Patents Act, 1988.
A CIP catalogue record for this book is available from
the British Library.
1 3 5 7 9 10 8 6 4 2
Printed in Great Britain

FREEDOM FLIGHT

BERNARD ASHLEY

ORCHARD BOOKS

I should like to thank Iris Ashley, George Hore,
Colin Izod, Megan Larkin and Jenny Nix
for their help with this book.
BA

CHAPTER ONE

Tom screwed his eyes through the sting of the whipped-up sea and held the Mirror dinghy into the waves. Mermaids he didn't believe in so it had to be a girl out there on the rocks. She was topless as best as he could see – and he was trying very hard to see – but her hair was short and dark, and no way was she leaning back and combing her tresses and calling him on to his doom. She was scurrying from one item of clothing to another on the small scraggy outcrop and turning them over to catch the rays of the sun – frantic and fidgety, glints of eye, and looking like a shipwreck victim herself.

But the son of a coastguard sees more than show-off girls who pretend Somerthorpe is the Costa del Sol; he sees tides running and waters rising fast and land that gets cut off twice a day; and this girl drying her clothes was in danger of never wearing them again if someone didn't get her off those rocks fast – be it coastguard or lifeboat or Tom Robinson Welton

5

himself. With no way of climbing the sheer cliff behind her, the girl had to be a dozo not to see that she would be under water in half an hour. Warning notices were as much use as words painted on the sea if stupid tourists didn't take any notice of them.

He swung the boom of his Mirror to starboard and changed course for the rocks. This way he could come alongside the spit of shingle and run aground for a few seconds while the girl jumped into the dinghy, if she was quick. It was her only chance in this sea; otherwise the flooding tide would carry her off fast like a twig along a gully.

He shouted at her. 'You! Girl on the rocks! Over here! I'm coming in!' But the girl didn't hear him against the sound of the sea, she frantically turned her clothes in the sun again. He shouted louder while he held the tiller firm in the rise and fall of the waves and headed *Sandpiper* for the spit he knew was there. Local knowledge. Some wouldn't have dared go in that close but Tom could have charted these waters. He wasn't up to much with words but with a mapping pen he was Christopher Blooming Columbus.

And despite the shine of the sun on the sea the girl must have seen him – because she suddenly grabbed at her clothes and disappeared behind a rock. As he came in on his sweep she ran out to him in the foaming water, pulling down a damp t-shirt over soggy jogging pants. She looked at him hard with sharp dark eyes and clambered shaking into the bottom of the boat, one gritty heap. And he could see straight off that this was no show-off holiday girl out on the rocks for a dare and ready to laugh off her ignorance of the local coast. She was frightened and shivering, still coughing on sea water, her black hair a tangle of sand and weed, her eyes big and scared, blinking all around her – and instead of arms flung around his neck and a salty kiss of thanks for the hero sailor, she huddled in the dinghy as if she was still naked, scared of being seen. *Distressed* was the word.

Tom yanked the foresheet to take the wind. 'You were dead lucky I saw you!' he shouted at her. 'Few more minutes and you'd be swep' off and under!'

But she stayed huddled down, didn't look up except for a quick look round at the open sea and a long swig from the bottle of water she grabbed up, not so much as a nod or a blink or a smile for him. *Cheers!* thought Tom. *Don't book the hall for the medal presentation!*

He'd beach the Mirror up above the water line in Seal Bay and show the girl the way back along the path to the promenade.

It was always exciting, beaching on the tide; there was a rush in the guts as the sail was dropped and the bow pointed at the beach. Riding in on a crest was like surfing but you had to hold the dinghy straight or she'd capsize and crack a mast. It was what Tom lived for, this thrill, this grip in the guts and the mastery of the manoeuvre. There was so much in life he couldn't do, but this he could.

'Hold on tight!' he shouted at the girl. 'Grab hold of the side!' But that meant her kneeling up, and she looked as if she wanted to stay huddling down, crouched in the well of the dinghy like a heap of old clothes. He was already coming in on a wave and he couldn't deviate and he couldn't spare a hand, he couldn't even look away from what he was doing – so he kicked her.

'*Srać!*' she shouted, like swearing at him in foreign. But if she didn't hold tight she'd be thrown about, could easily crack her head on the boom; and there's nothing more dangerous than being knocked out in the sea not wearing a life jacket.

Anyhow, she understood the kick; she grabbed the gunwale.

'Brace yourself!' he shouted. As the surge of the wave took them roaring in she grabbed at the sides and held on with her head down. The mainsail fell around her as Tom steered the dinghy at right angles to the wave, and swept up the slope of Seal Bay.

'All change, please! Take all your belongings with

you.' In a second Tom was out of the craft and round at the bow, pulling it away from the suck of the last wave. 'Come on! Pay your way!' And, copying him, the girl climbed out and helped, eyes still everywhere. She stopped pulling as soon as they were clear of the surf, but Tom had to get above the high water mark or his boat would float off at full tide. 'Keep going! Come on, up there!' She muttered something but he pointed and they pulled together to a high spot in soft sand.

'There!' he said to the girl. 'And don't you be shy about saying thanks!' She was white with dark skin, not bad looking, and in one of his fantasies a grateful kiss wouldn't have spoiled his dinner. But all she did was flash her eyes around in every direction at once before suddenly throwing herself onto the sand, exhausted.

Tom bent over and patted her, cautiously. 'Don't worry. You're safe now. We'll find your mum and dad...' And he stood back watching till she finally pulled herself to her feet. 'I'll take you along to the town,' he said. 'Do what you like, then...' She had a couple of old bruises on her arms as if she worked at something physical; she definitely didn't look like a holidaymaker, but she might be from the fairground up the coast; her drying hair had curled and she held her head up proud, like a gypsy girl.

'Not to hurry!' she snapped at him, her eyes still

everywhere. Apart from the swear word it was the first time she'd spoken; her voice was clipped, definitely a foreigner speaking English.

'I can't not hurry. I've got my own problems. Come on!'

'Then you go!' She waved him away like a princess with a serf, still urgently looking this way and that. But there was only this way, no that, not for walking. The choice was a sheer drop one side and a narrow path on the other. Behind the bay was a beet field with a barbed wire fence running along its edge, leading north to the edge of the holiday town – the only way to go.

'You got no option. We go along here, then you c'n peel off into the town.' He set off on the path back towards the beach huts and the main holiday beach. But he made sure he kept a few steps ahead of her: who knew, one of his mates might see him and spread the word. Kids who got off with summer visitors were lepers in the winter.

But no one passed them as they went around the headland and started walking north towards the main promenade, the world quiet and empty, just the close throb of a vessel in the shipping lane heading into Lowestoft. The girl trailed those few steps behind – now he realised that she'd got no footwear, but she walked on the stony path as if her feet were leather, slowing when he slowed, speeding up when he did, jumping around as she checked where they were going, looking about her as if she might run off somewhere any second. He kept his head down himself, dark hair blown all ways and allowed to stay, his eyes slits, his wide mouth – great for grinning – pursed up tight right now. If she didn't want to be seen, neither did he; and if she wanted to clear off that was all right by him.

In no time, on his right was the holidaymakers' Fore Beach, patches of sand between the shingle, on his left was the first line of beach huts with his own family's chalet, *Beaufort* – and an empty space behind it where *Sandpiper* should have been berthed. They were still 300 metres from the harbour area where he could point her to go before he dived off about his own business...

...And – oh no! – who suddenly had to be coming along the line of huts towards them but Charlie Gull, the beach hut man! In his council cap he strutted the promenade like a one-man military patrol. And he knew Tom and he knew Tom's dad – he patrolled along as far as the coastguard station every hour; and there wasn't much he didn't spot in the small seaside town, from couples cuddling behind groynes to wind-surfers stacking their boards where they shouldn't. Tom stopped dead at the sight of the man, ready to dive inside *Beaufort*, because he was supposed to be at home; and the way you treated mums you couldn't treat dads. And his dad would definitely be told he was down here, Charlie's mouth was as loose as a split bag of flour. Tom went for the beach hut door, the key out of his pocket; but this time the girl didn't stop short. She suddenly ran up the chalet steps and grabbed hold of Tom.

'Come, to me!' She twisted him to stand in front of her, took his face in her hands and kissed him full on the lips.

The shock of it took his breath, fizzed his blood, rang a couple of bells. He had to pull off to breathe. 'So you're grateful?' he managed. But what a place for such gratitude, out here in front of the world! He put a steadying hand to the beach hut door as Charlie Gull muttered under his breath and stood staring at them.

'Go in!' The girl pulled Tom's hand down towards the lock and urged with her fingers for the door to be opened. He did it as quickly as he could and they fell into the beach hut, the girl rattling the door locked behind them.

'What's all that about?' Tom stared at her. 'Are you after my body?' And he half meant it – because, what *was* she up to, that was no polite thank-you kiss. And who was she?

'You know me!' She looked out of the scrag of net curtain by the door, turned and poked at her chest. 'I am friend!'

'Friend?' Tom eyed her. What was her game? With her European sort of looks and bare gypsy feet he'd half thought fairground, someone on the move; now she was definitely illegal immigrant – jumped off a ship coming into Lowestoft, claiming she knew him. But, no way – he had to get her out of here so he could go off to sort his own problems, he hadn't got the time to be her friend right now. She was looking this way and that out of the window, her fingers agitating at a small silver bird on a chain round her neck.

From outside, the sounds of the Saturday beach invaded the thin walls of the hut; the slight suck of the sea overlaid by familiar shouts and chases and shocked wet screams, everything sounding so normal. And Tom Robinson Welton was stuck with an illegal immigrant!

Now she turned to him. Her eyes were big and proud in the dark hut, but he couldn't stop a look at the lips that had kissed him. What did this girl want from him? Could it be what he'd like from her, perhaps another kiss?

'You saved me, I thank you.' Said softly; but now her voice growled in a threat as she pushed her face closer to his. 'If you do not help me, you still do not go against me! You do nothing!'

'Best thing I'm good at.'

She seemed content with that. She crouched in a corner, stayed silent as if she were used to doing that. Outside, Charlie Gull was making leather noises with the straps of his ticket machine, his belt and his walkie-talkie case, he did it all the time. Tom could picture him, hanging about, an eye on the sinful beach hut with Tom and a girl in it.

The girl kept quiet, but Tom was one of those people who had to fill an awkward silence. After what seemed the length of three English lessons he had to ask her in a whisper, 'What do you need help for?'

She shrugged. 'This man, a driver, he brings us in England. Who cares what happens to people like us?'

So Tom was right – and he knew what she was on about. The way locals talked about the cheap immigrant labour on the sugar beet farms they sounded like some other form of life.

'Where d'you come from?' he asked her.

'Warszawa. Warsaw. Poland.'

Tom took a quick look out of the window. Charlie Gull was still hovering. If he knew what was in here he'd turn her in as quick as issuing a ticket.

There was another long silence, the girl still crouching, Tom not moving, until he heard someone speak to Charlie Gull from along the promenade and the man moved off.

'You're a good old way from home!' he said to the girl. 'Well, you're right in the shite and I'll help you if I can – but it's got to be quick. So how come you fetched up on those rocks, drank half the North Sea?'

The girl looked hard at Tom. 'I go back to Poland. I have friends, one special, her family is good. I run secret to the ship, hide, but when the ship goes out, a sailor, he sees me.' She shrugged at him. 'And what will they do when they take me back to the port?'

'Lowestoft police station, refugee camp. They'll get the driver in, and—'

'And this trucker, he *looks*, he is at the docks.' She poked herself hard with a quivering finger. 'The ship people know him, they will give me back to him.'

'And you don't like him?'

The girl's answer was to mime a spit on the floor. 'So – I jump from the ship—'

'Into the North Sea! 'Strewth! That's drastic! That's cold, winter and summer.'

'I take life jacket and I take the chance.' She shrugged, and the little silver bird danced. 'I jump and I think, I can drown, but I will do so, die first, not go back to him.'

''Strewth!' Poor kid, she was desperate; and didn't it put Tom's problems in their miserable place?

'You are one hell good sailor!' she said, out of the blue.

'Thanks.' Tom smiled, and looked her in the eye, sincere and true. 'I'll help you if I can. But you've got to work around me. First things first, I'll get you something to eat.'

The girl nodded, she'd accept. No more thanks.

'What's your name?' he asked.

'Anna.' But she stared at him too hard; and he knew that she was lying. 'No, this is lie – ' She thought better of it. 'Anna is *Matka,* my mother. Was. Me, I am Danuta. She calls me Danni.'

'Right, Danni. I won't be long. You stay hidden till I get back.'

She shot out a hand and grabbed his arm, hard and hurting. She was tough. 'You come back?' This was more a growl. 'You only, not with police?'

'I'm on your side, Danni, OK?'

'I have to believe.'

'Well, do believe. Now, listen, no one from my house is going to come down here today, but there's other chalets, little huts, loads of people around...so don't make any noise.'

She looked him in the eye, a cold glint. 'People like me do not,' she said, before pulling herself behind some deck chairs. She knew the hiding game.

Tom went, but he made sure not to lock the door

behind him: because in spite of what he was doing and saying, in spite of the kiss, there was just a glint of hope in his mind that this fiery girl wouldn't be here when he came back. Like having a bad dream he wanted to wake up from her, only have to worry about himself – so why not give her an easy way of escape? She was going to be real trouble, this girl, and the trouble he was in was bad enough already. More than.

CHAPTER TWO

Tom slowed and slowed and slowed as he came back to the beach hut from the refreshments kiosk. He'd taken his time going and choosing, and now he was taking it coming back. He surely was in enough trouble already. It kept running and running through his mind.

'Get away! Get out of it!'

A ball bounces, anger bounces, and books bounce if they're thrown hard enough. That morning Tom's school dictionary had hit the living room wall full on the edge of its spine and come halfway back at him. As he'd jerked aside to avoid it, his writing had spun to the floor the wrong side down and smudged his still wet attempt at spelling 'squadron'.

'There's no bloody "w" – it's a trick!'

His mother had come in from the kitchen like a teacher at a fight. 'Oi! You leave that out, boy! I only told you to *try!* I said I'd help, didn't I?'

But the help Tom wanted wasn't hers, it was God's,

help with the puzzle that Tom Robinson Welton was always fighting to solve: a puzzle Tom's little sister Sally had cracked at Nursery School – reading and writing; what they called 'Literacy'.

'Stupid war! Stupid history project!' Tom had picked up the notebook and crumpled it into an origami cabbage. 'Who cares about Somerthorpe Past, it was bloody yonks ago! Holiday's holiday! I get enough of this all year!' And still clutching the mangled notebook, he'd thrown his face down into his arm and cried out his misery in great sobs.

'Come on Tom, boy, you know what your father said: put some time in. An' crying don't help,' his mother told him. 'Leave out the drama, you just get an hour's work done then you can get off out of it.'

But Tom had lifted his head slowly and sworn at her, the unacceptable 'f' word, telling his father where to go – and said slowly to give it real meaning – and while she'd taken the deepest of God's breaths and watched him in despairing disgust, he'd yanked himself up from the table and slammed past her out of the house – to go out in *Sandpiper* on his own, not wearing his life jacket because that way he was defying his mother and his father, and anyway, if anything happened to a hopeless case like him, who cared? Let him drown. No one could be worse off in this world than a kid who couldn't learn.

Except, perhaps, this girl, right now. But please smile, God, and let her be gone. She was probably some lying fairground girl who was kidding him along – out on the rocks with a boy who'd swum ashore and left her. So the result he wanted was that she'd gone away; then he could get himself home and make it up with his mum before his dad came in.

Yes, he hoped like hell she hadn't landed on his plate.

He knocked at the beach-hut door and let himself in to the gloom. But instantly there was the squeak of a deck chair moving. She hadn't gone. Shit!

'Great! You're still here,' he said. He gave her the Mars bar – which she tore at fast. He fizzed open the can of drink which she quickly drank, and burped on, no apology, just crushed the can.

'How bad is he, this man?'

'You think I lie to you?' She raised her voice at him, and her eyes blazed in the gloom.

'No, it's just, I need to know, if I'm going to help you... An' keep it down if you don't mind.'

In the beach hut on the left a family renting by the week had just come off the sand and were brewing up for lunch, putting their deck chairs out on the veranda. On the other side old Mrs MacKenzie, a local, would soon be down with her *Daily Mail* till it was time for tea.

'He is...monster!' Her hands were clutching down her t-shirt, twisting it violently from side to side.

'So, where d'you live?' Tom pushed on.

'Lowestoft. He is trucker for Polish transport people.' She looked as if she might spit on the floor for real.

Tom knew the yellow cabs and trailers from Gdansk, coming out of Lowestoft port. They were bright, you couldn't miss them. 'English?'

Danni nodded.

'You speak good English.'

'Why not?' She shot a look at him as if he might be treating her like a little kid. 'I learn in school. A little.'

'Yeah, me too. A little. So what do you want to do, Danni? Another try at a ship?' Because this was taking time, and time was running out for Tom to do what *he* wanted, to get that apology in to his mother and a page more project done before he raced back to Seal Bay for the dinghy; otherwise his dad would have to know about him throwing a strop and sailing illegal.

'Yes, ship. I want Poland. I want not to go back to him – ever!'

'You go back where you came from?'

She looked at him sideways, sort of, could she trust him? The answer must have been a cautious yes. 'I go back to friends, people I know, streets of Warsaw. And *he* is not there...' She shuddered.

'Where's your mum, then? You said her name *was* Anna…'

Danni folded her arms at him. 'She is dead.'

'Ah.' Things were getting a little bit clearer. 'And you're alone with this man?'

'No!' She almost snapped off his head. 'He has sister.'

'All right!' But, *the poor kid!* was what Tom was thinking. An illegal immigrant, on the run and alone in the world with only a friend and her family to run to. But at least she'd got them. 'I don't blame you, if your mum's dead and there's people you know over there.' Tom suddenly gripped her slender shoulders and stood off with his arms straight. She looked so vulnerable that he suddenly wanted to kiss her, and to cuddle her for comfort. But violently she shook him off. 'Srać!' she growled.

So forget kissing. Get rid! 'I'll see you back to Lowestoft, it's easy from here.' Lowestoft was a few miles north, a busy old place – and she'd got on a ship once already, it was people coming in they were worried about, not going out.

'He is looking for me. My mother – Matka – yes, she is dead; but he still wants servant. Tom…'

Tom looked at the girl. He could well believe that; he'd heard about illegal people coming in who had to work like skivvies to keep protected.

'Right. So you stay here and I'll come back as quick as I can and help sort you out.' He pointed to the hiding place behind the deck chair. 'You hide and I'll be back before you know it.' He turned away, and then back again. 'Here, how d'you know my name?'

Like a cocky teacher showing a thick student – and he was well used to that – she pointed to the row of mugs on the wall. 'The name is here.' Sally had written everyone's name above their mug hooks.

'You're sharp! Well, you can trust Tom Robinson Welton. He's not up to doing a lot of stuff, but he does follow through.' And without waiting for any reaction from her, he said, 'See you soon,' and went out of the door and shut it behind him...

...To walk blind smack into Philip Swain.

Philip Swain!

Philip Bloody Swain – the enemy, Emma Thorpe's cousin who lived with her and her family, fostered. Emma, the girl who Tom had fancied since Juniors and who lived in the manor house the other side of the church, loads of money, dogs and a horse. Living near, he often found himself coming home from school with her, and he sometimes got to go over to her place with keys and cleaning stuff because his mum did regular housework there. And he'd kissed her once in a game at a party. Whether this Philip fancied her too Tom didn't know – except he wouldn't put anything past him; he'd use any leg-up he could. He wasn't big, he wasn't tough, he could have been flattened by Tom any time Tom was in the mood for getting yuck on his hands; but he had this stoaty way of talking, all hidden passages and creaking floorboards in his tricky mind that made him sound like he knew stuff he shouldn't. Swain only had to look at Tom and Tom felt as if he'd got a dirty nose or he hadn't done up his zip. Yes, Philip Swain was definitely the last person Tom wanted to meet right now.

'It's Thom-as!' That, too – he *would* bloody call him 'Thom-as'; the last bit almost like *arse*.

'Oh, hiya, Phil.' Big surprise! Act big surprise.

'You look a bit furtive. What have you been up to in there?'

'Nothing! Just sorting out some stuff.'

'Oh, yeah?' Philip Swain had that look on his face – always – that made Tom doubt his own name.

'Yeah, sorting new lines for the dinghy. Had to beach her over Seal Bay.'

'And you haven't got one – after your sorting out? A line?' Swain's cocky expression said that he was noticing everything, including Tom's hands being empty.

"S'right, I've got to fetch one from home.'

'Ah.'

'So what are you up to?' Tom started walking away from the beach hut, along the promenade towards the town steps; that had to be the way Philip was heading, too.

'Reading, and sorting out some research stuff.' Philip flipped back an intellectual lock of hair and sniffed through his sharp nose, holding up a thick book, a students' A4 block of paper and his mobile phone. 'Projects don't get done by wishful thinking, Thom-as. We read, interview, ask, phone – go beyond the word – enjoy the research, in which way the summer holiday can be enjoyed to the max.'

Tom looked at him. A kick to the balls would be enjoyed to the max right now.

Philip suddenly stopped, so Tom had to stop as well. 'Hold on, Thom-as! I've just thought of something, Dozo...'

So what the hell could that be?

'...You didn't lock your beach hut. You just came skulking out of it and shut the door, no key...' With a superior smile, his nose tilted up level with his forehead, Philip turned away from the town steps. 'What if someone undesirable got in?'

Tom had to run to catch him up, going back. ''S'all right, I haven't got the key, that's why. I left it at the dinghy – yeah, Dozo, I know. Only, don't say anything, Phil...'

Philip stopped. 'Oh, dear,' he said, shaking his head. 'You really are stupid, aren't you?'

'Yeah.' And in silence they walked to the steps again and into the small holiday town. And at that moment Tom realised that if he were going to help the Polish girl in any way, it would have to be up against sharp-eyed smart arses like Philip Swain.

CHAPTER THREE

Tom lived a wanting sort of life. He wanted to be able to read better, he wanted to be able to write properly, he wanted his dad to give him the attention he gave to little Sally, more than the grudging grunts Tom got because he was half good in boats. And he wanted to have something more serious to do with Emma Thorpe, but she always seemed out of his class. She was pretty, with big eyes, a sexy smile and long fair hair that smelt of strawberry when you got that close. Just now and again, rarely but nice, she and Tom lassooed each other with laughs, but it was princess and favoured footman stuff – he would have liked being just more *level*. His mother cleaned for her mother twice a week and got shopping in for her when Mrs Thorpe was too busy being a financial consultant. And that boss and worker thing gave Emma a sort of click-the-fingers way with him. And there was her quickness with things. She knew her way round a computer like Technical Support at PC

World, while Tom's spelling fingers always seemed to get tied in knots. If she let him share a bit of homework on her Packard Bell she clicked the mouse too fast for Tom even to read the options.

She was out of his league so it was without any real reason that Tom didn't want Emma to know that he'd got a girl in his beach hut – quite apart from Danni being illegal – not until he'd helped her and he could safely talk about it. And to do that, first he had to make his peace at home.

He needn't have panicked. His mother had gone out of the house to clean the church hall, taken Sally with her. She came back to find him sweating at his books.

'That's better, boy,' she went on, 'that's my old Tom, who tries.' But something more had to be said right now and it had to be Tom who said it.

'I'm sorry, Mum, about…before.'

She looked at him with a mix of tears and tick-off in her eyes, was about to say something when the telephone suddenly rang. Tom picked it up. If it was his dad – and it usually was – he wouldn't mind the man knowing he was here at home hitting the books.

'Fiveseveneightfive.'

'Your mother there?' Yes, it was his dad: no 'Hiya Tom, boy!'

'I can just see her the other side of this big pile of school books.'

'Well, give her a message. You can give a simple message, can't you?'

The man didn't see the two fingers of Tom's simple message back.

'Tell her I'm gonna be late, don't put my meal on. We've got a mystery on the go.'

'What film are you watching?'

'Ha, ha. There's been an alert. Girl in the sea, jumped ship last night but no body found yet. Probably one of these asylum illegal lot. Can't stand down till we know our bit of the coast is clean.'

Clean! Of dirty Danni. Refugees had to be dirty, didn't they?

'So I'll see you when I see you, tell your mother.'

'OK.'

'Got that?'

Tom hung up. So they knew about the girl, the ship had radioed, they were searching for her – or her body. He'd have to let her know: but he also had to get *Sandpiper* berthed.

'Your dad, was it?' his mother asked.

'Yeah, he's gonna be late. Getting drunk, then having an afternoon in bed with Dockyard Dora.'

'So long as I know.' Tom's mother went to turn down the oven. When she came back, Tom had gone.

'Got much further?' she asked the scribbly pages as she stacked his books. And she took them to his room, shaking her head.

Sailing in from Seal Bay, Tom pulled the dinghy on its trolley along behind the line of beach huts to its berth. A quick run for fish and chips and cola, then a polite wave to Mrs MacKenzie on one side and the renters on the other and he was in with Danni again.

And she looked so different! She'd been sorting herself out. She'd found a red linen napkin and tied it around her head, workers' headscarf style; somehow she'd smoothed the damp creases of her t-shirt which showed her figure now; and she'd found some Sun Factor Four and rubbed it into her face and arms, giving her a more holidaymaker look, easier for getting about. She looked sexy and older as her sharp eyes checked that he'd not brought the law with him.

'My dad says – he's a coastguard – my dad says they're looking for you. They don't know whether you're alive and kicking or at the bottom of the North Sea...'

Danni looked at him. 'Bottom of the sea is good!' she said. And her stare and a quick smile which flipped his stomach told him what he'd known since his father's phone call. Without doubt he had got himself a second holiday task. And whichever way he played it, he had to hide up this girl till next morning – while the authorities searched and a trucker prowled.

'Listen, this man,' he asked her, 'what's he look like? In case I see him?'

Danni twisted her face. 'Him?' She shut her eyes, her body seemed to shrink as she crushed her fish and chips paper and shuddered. '*Him* is *Harry.*'

'And he weren't – he wasn't your dad?'

'*Never! Never!*' Said like an explosion in the confined space. 'I have no father...not since baby.' Flying bits of fish and outrage.

'Ah.' Tom wanted to know more about all that – although, no, he didn't; he knew too much already.

The girl took a swig of drink. 'Matka says it is our good luck that he comes from here. She say she wants this part in England when we go out of Poland... Huh! Our luck!' She suddenly came at him like a dagger. '*Bad* luck!'

'Anyhow, what's he look like?' Tom crumpled his fish and chips paper into the plastic bag he'd brought.

Her eyes were slits now. 'Like fish, slippy fish, stare-you eyes, cod mouth...'

'I'll spot him!'

'Matka goes with him because it's very bad for us in Warszawa. She is trusting him.'

'Yeah. Well, you never really know people till

31

they're indoors.' But the time was skidding round his watch face and he didn't have to be missed at home for much longer; he'd got to move this on. Meanwhile, no one from the family would be down to the beach this late. So just for tonight she'd be all right here, although she'd have to be quiet, and he'd have to get her away first thing in the morning when no one was about. The council was strict about people sleeping in beach huts – but tonight the risk had to be worth it, if Danni could keep as still and as quiet as a resting moth.

Tom wrapped up her rubbish with his. 'You sleep here, OK? You've got a lilo blown up over there and you lie behind the deck chairs so no one can see you through the keyhole. If it's cold there's towels for blankets.' He pointed to them; and he felt himself go red as he added the next bit. 'An' there's a seaside bucket for – in the night. Anything else you'll have to go down to the sea. Now –' going on quickly '– the key. Lock yourself in, and in the morning I'll knock the old V for victory to say it's me.'

'What *victory*?' When she didn't understand her face could look so cross.

'V for victory. Morse code.' It was what his dad used on the back door when he came in late, dot, dot, dot – dash; light, light, light – heavy. Tom did it for Danni.

'OK. Then we go to Lowestoft?' she demanded.

'Yup. We go to Lowestoft. Tomorrow. Early.'

She looked at him straight and long, her body very still except for a swelling of her breast as she sat up and took him by surprise. 'You are good guy!'

And Tom had a new and sudden want to kiss her again. But before he did anything so stupid, he made a move, and went. He heard her lock the door behind him and ran off along the promenade already thinking of bus routes or possibly bikes to Lowestoft. Whatever, he was determined to help that illegal girl back in the chalet.

And straight off finding out how easy it is to run into complications; like Emma Thorpe, cycling down Glebe Lane at the top of the town.

'Tom!'

'Emm!' And did she look good! Short summer shorts, a narrow halter top showing her belly; blonde hair tied up in a ribbon – a sight he'd flip over to see. Normally. But today he groaned.

'You all right?' she called. 'Having a reasonable holiday?' She stopped and leant back off her saddle, combed her fingers through non-existent tangles in her hair.

'Yeah, great!' And part of him wanted to blurt out everything, how it wasn't great at all and how he'd got this problem she could help him with. But still part of him wanted to keep it quiet.

'Heard you needed a new line.'

'That's right. Halyard.' So Philip Swain had been talking already.

Emma suddenly snapped her fingers. 'I've been thinking...'

'That's a mistake – it's holidays, give your brain a break.'

'Tomorrow...'

'Sunday, all day.'

'My mother's riding Molly at the Fressingfield Show. But she's taking the bigger horsebox, so Molly's in one side and there's room for bikes in the other...' Emma's face seemed bright with the plan. 'Someone needs to be there to help with hitching and unhitching the trailer – which could be you, couldn't it? But you don't have to stay once she's unhitched and set up; we could go for a ride round if you like.'

'Great!' Tom said – as a twist of some new acid fizzed inside him. The beautiful Emma Thorpe was inviting him on a day out that every hairy bloke in his school would've killed for. 'Yeah, sounds great!' He tried to blink his eyes in excitement, but one eyelid ran slow.

'It's early, but I expect you can get up for half past six...'

Tom looked away and back again. Why did life

have to be so *complicated*? Why couldn't he go back to being five years old when his biggest worry was progressing from Velcro to laces? Nothing was ever going to work out for him, was it? Tom Robinson Welton was never meant to have a day without grief. Why couldn't God let him get the Polish girl into Lowestoft docks one day and go off on Emma's treat another day – because he *had* to help Danni, she was down there hiding in his beach hut. But, shame, guilt, blushing at the thought, for some reason he still couldn't make it right by bringing Emma in on it. He could have told her everything, he'd got nothing to be ashamed of; Danni had landed in his lap, he hadn't gone looking for her. But still something inside him wanted Danni kept as his secret...

'Well, no...' So this was when he had to lie like a spy. 'What a rotten shame! Oh, no! What a pisser!'

'What?' Emma frowned.

'I've gone and fixed up something for tomorrow...'

'Oh.' Pretty girls aren't often refused things. 'Well, never mind. Just a thought.' She kicked back her pedal ready to push off.

'Yeah, I'm sailing. I'm showing *Sandpiper* to someone. Some kid on holiday. I only just fixed it up.'

'You don't have to make excuses. You've got your life.' Emma turned in the road and faced home. 'Phil can do it.' She tugged down at her halter top and a stone of disappointment dropped heavy in Tom's stomach.

'Emm, I only wish I could...'

'Sure.' And Emma Thorpe hitched up onto her saddle and cycled off; strawberry hair in its summer bow, smooth tanned back showing the straight light line of her spine, long legs, this beautiful girl who'd offered him a day out together on their own – and Tom Robinson Welton had had to refuse it!

He stood watching her go wheeling off past the church and swore in a fit of angry guilt for lying. Rotten life! Perhaps Danni's mother and all the dead in those churchyard graves were the lucky ones!

CHAPTER FOUR

Bus – it would have to be a bus to Lowestoft. Somerthorpe didn't have its own railway station – visitors coming by rail went to Lowestoft and caught the bus. And bikes were out because there was only Tom's own that wasn't flat-tyred and rusty-chained.

He crept out of the house, sharing the early summer morning with the birds and the watering jets on the fields of sugar beet. It was a time of day Tom liked, once he was up and into it: sailors set their times by tides, not by clocks and he was used to early starts with his father, on those rare days when there was space for him. Tom had left a brief note. *Out. Bissy.* Carrying a plastic shopping bag he felt like a runaway with a bag of biscuits, apples, a carton of orange juice, a pair of his old trainers, and a hooded sweatshirt to disguise the Polish girl. And money: he'd gone into his birthday box and loaned himself a few notes.

The cottage where Tom lived was about fifty metres from the church, and along the side of the church ran Glebe Lane, the way to Emma Thorpe's big house; and even the sight of the way to Emma's suddenly started up his stomach again – that weird feeling of loss and guilt all mixed up like being scared and hungry at the same time. He'd never felt so miserable nor so duty driven. And another kick where it hurt. If he thought he'd have the promenade to himself at six-thirty on a Sunday morning he was wrong. He hadn't expected Charlie Gull to be about so soon. As Tom crossed the empty road and ran down the steps to the promenade, there the man stood with his walkie-talkie to his ear.

'Ah!' Seeing Tom he switched it off. 'Where's your dad?' The man's rumpled eyes looked back up the steps behind Tom as if he might be following.

'In bed. He was late last night, won't be sailing today.'

'I'm not talking about sailing, boy.' The tall old man hitched and pulled at his official bits and pieces, the keys on his council belt, his radio, the peak of his cap. 'Got some news for him.'

'What's that?'

Charlie Gull took him by surprise. 'Did he tell you about that female, jumped off the timber ship...?'

'Yes...'

'Well, she ain't dead, boy, she was seen, out on the rocks. An' a boat, a dinghy's been seen taking her off.

Mirror, red sail. A fellow with binoculars in hut thirty-three seen it. Part of the plan no doubt...'

'What plan?' Hell! He'd been seen! But a lot of the small stuff that sailed these waters was Mirrors with their red sails, the junior yacht club was a Mirror club, it was a bit like saying you'd seen a Ford on the A12.

'What plan, boy? Aliens! Illegals. Bringing 'em ashore. I'm gonna see if he got the number off the sail. Or the name on the side.' Charlie rubbed his full morning nose. 'Even if it weren't a plan, the bloke who took her off the rocks might know where she went...'

'You're right, Charlie, he might.' Tom's head had gone into a spin like a three-sixty capsize. He could be identified by the number on his sail! Philip Swain and Emma Thorpe knew he'd been sailing, and other people had seen him pull the trolley up the beach, plus Charlie Gull had seen him kissing a strange girl and go into *Beaufort* with her. So she could be traced, through him!

'I've left a message up the Coastguard. Reckon they can call off their search, seaward. It's police business now. Immigration, boy.' Charlie Gull made the word sound like a dose of poison. ''Less you're going home an' you can tell him?'

'No, not for a bit. I've come down to do some maintenance on the dinghy.'

'Oh, yes?' Charlie Gull started hitching and clipping himself together again. 'Going sailing again?'

Again? Again? 'Might do,' Tom said. 'Halyard. Gotta go.' And he ran off along the promenade towards the girl – to get her out of that beach hut fast, somewhere away from Charlie Gull.

He gave his special V for victory knock and the door was cautiously opened. She pulled him in, shut the door.

'Is late!' she accused him.

'Is early! Bloody early, thanks!' he said. 'Put these on.' He gave her the trainers. 'And this.' He tossed her the sweatshirt. 'Pull that hood up an' walk like a boy, we've got to get out of here.'

Muttering something in Polish she pulled on the trainers and slid the sweatshirt over her head, while Tom quickly tidied the beach hut.

'They saw you. Us. Someone saw me take you off the rocks in the boat. Well, they don't know it's me for certain, not yet, but they know you're not drowned. So now it's police and immigration on the hunt.'

She looked this way, she looked that. Her legs and her feet couldn't keep still as if she were itching to go. But she stopped in a strange moment of calm. 'You tell me –' she asked him out of nowhere '– how boys they walk?'

'I don't know.' He ruffled his hair. 'Sort of manly, I

s'pose.' He strutted a pace like a Principal Boy in a pantomime.

'Manly. I know *manly*,' she growled. She was still looking at him. 'Old manly, young manly. I walk like you.'

'Yeah. Well. Please yourself.' She had suddenly fluttered Tom's heart but he didn't know why. 'We're going to get the bus to Lowestoft before they get any real searching going on the roads. Then you can skulk around the shops till you make a run for a ship, there'll be tons of people about...'

'I know what I have to do.'

'Good. Then off we go before some early birds come down to the beach...' He pulled the hood up tighter to her face, took a chance and tucked her dark curling hair into it, as well as the little silver bird on its chain. She stared at him, expressionless. After a quick look along the promenade, he ushered her out of the door. She jumped out and jogged on the veranda like a morning runner while he locked the beach hut and hid the key. He tried to put an arm round her shoulder as if she were an old mate, but she shook him off. 'Srać!'

They ran to the first gap in the huts, through to the High Street and along to the bus depot – round the last corner to be suddenly blanked by its big double doors shut tight. Overnight, two single deckers sat inside, but never were the doors shut in daylight.

'*Zdolny!* Where buses?'

Tom swore. He looked around, listened at the door, wanted to start thumping on the woodwork. But the girl was at the timetable in its frame on the wall.

'"Sunday,"' she read out, 'is 13:10, 15:10, 17:10.'

'Bollocks! That's five, six hours to wait!'

She stared at him. 'So we walk!' No buses suddenly seemed a small problem to a girl prepared to cross Europe.

'No way! Too far.' Tom leant against the doors. What a smack in the face! And what a dozo he was, not checking on Sunday bus times before he started on this. He always prided himself on his planning for the dinghy; he reckoned at least if he wasn't clever he was practical – and now he wasn't that, either!

'We not walk, then what we do?' Danni was shooting looks up and down the street.

'OK. I'll tell you – when I've thought of something.' But right now Tom Robinson Welton's head was as shut as that blank depot door.

'Bike,' Danni said; 'you have bike?'

'I've got *a* bike. One…'

'Enough. For me.'

Sure, a bike for her was the next obvious option – but she was wrong; he told her they'd have to steal another one. Two of them out for a Sunday ride would look much less suspicious when there was a police and immigration search on. It was only a pity that Emma and Philip Swain had taken theirs to Fressingfield because the Thorpe house was empty this morning, he could have borrowed one from there.

And suddenly Tom had it. A new plan. *The Thorpe place was empty this morning!* Once Danni got to Lowestoft what would she have to do? Hide up again, lose herself in the holidaymakers till it was dark enough to head for a ship. Then why not hide up for some of that time at this end and get the bus when it did decide to run? Emma Thorpe and her mother and Philip Swain had gone to Fressingfield for the whole day with the horse, which left the stable empty – so couldn't they use that? The more Tom thought about it, the more possible it seemed. Emma's father led a separate life from the others, lived somewhere else, and while the dogs would still be about, Tom knew them well and they knew him: they'd bark at him once and then trot off – and if Danni was with him they'd accept her, too.

'Got it! Come on, Dan! I know where we're going. Somewhere safe for a bit. Till we get the bus...'

'We go now!'

'We don't. We wait. Trust me. Forget bikes. We hide up this end instead of Lowestoft, simple. Safer, really, with your man living there.'

'He is not my man!' Danni turned for her eyes to scorch him.

'You know what I mean. Listen, I've got a good place, you'll be all right there for a few hours.'

'Me, just? Not you?'

'We'll see. If I can be doing other useful stuff to help us I'll be doing it…'

'Then we go? We go today!' Not a question – a fierce statement of fact.

'Yeah, we go today, *together*. Can't you see – you won't stand out with me along.'

She shrugged, and then suddenly she wasn't there; she was down at his feet with her hands over her head. Because a deafening noise was shaking the street as a helicopter came clattering low across the rooftops – like warfare, like something filled with snipers who knew what they were looking for: a yellow RAF Sea King. Tom had been up in it, and he knew how well those Rescue people could see through their powerful binoculars when they were on a land-sea search, how their heat-seeking apparatus could track a human body, how their computer could pinpoint a location.

'Stay still!'

'Srać!' Danni was crouched at the foot of the wall, huddled the way she'd been in the dinghy, her hood held up tight to her face.

In the sky, the Sea King banked and took a sweep south along the sands towards Seal Bay.

'Come on!' said Tom. 'Get out from under 'fore it comes back.'

'He looks for me?' Danni stayed huddled.

'I reckon. Could be.'

'Yellow! Same colour as Gdansk trucks.' And keeping her head down, she got up and ran with Tom.

Running, he didn't have to talk; he could keep ahead, lead the way, and he could think; ask himself why he was doing this. Why was he helping some girl he didn't know to get away from a man he didn't know and go to a life he didn't know and couldn't imagine? Why? Why wasn't he cycling around Fressingfield with the luscious Emma?

Why?

And as he ran he knew that part of the answer was what had happened yesterday outside the beach hut. The kiss. The real kiss, the deep kiss, the sexy kiss. He was helping this girl for his own selfish ends; she'd done it once, she could do it again. Being kissed like that made a kid like him feel a bit more the ticket. Young manly. Yup, he liked that. So he was helping the girl. Simple.

That was it, wasn't it?

CHAPTER FIVE

Tom was used to being around here at the side of Emma's house. When he brought something over for his mother's cleaning, he came here sometimes to stroke Molly the mare's head and give her sugar, showing a bit of interest in the Thorpe world – so he knew the geography of the place; and now he made straight for it. Ears alert for where the Sea King was, they'd turned just short of Tom's row of cottages and along Glebe Lane to the manor house. At the gate the dogs had been no bother at all, then he'd taken the girl around to the outhouses. At the side of the stable there was a small tack room with saddles, reins, and horse blankets. After a last ever-so-innocent look around, he opened the door and they ducked inside.

'How long? We stay here how long?' Danni wanted to know, sharp eyes, tilted chin, feet forever on the move – in the door and out, staring up at the sky and across the church grounds to the road.

'Till the time for the bus.' She hadn't got a watch

so he checked. 'Five hours, max.'

She blew out her cheeks, looked round the dingy tack room. 'Then we go to Lowestoft? For sure?' She flicked her fingers with a crack.

'That's it, and mix in with people and do holiday sorts of things till it's really dark.'

Danni was staring at Tom with eyes that said she was making up her mind about something. 'This Harry – in Lowestoft, he looks for me…'

'So I'll help you; that's why I'm coming. If he knows you got on a ship and jumped off her, if he hears the news and finds out you were rescued off a rock by a dinghy… *Then* he looks for you in Lowestoft.'

'He will know. He want me back, bad.'

'Yeah?' And now the big question. 'Why's that, then?' He held his stare as Danni's eyes narrowed. Would she say more, or not? *Was* she what she said she was, or was she some girl run off from home in London or Cambridge or Birmingham?

She looked him back in the eyes, all of ten long seconds. 'Very bad thing, I have done,' she said.

'Yeah? What's that?'

'*Very* bad thing.'

'OK.' Was she making up some more to keep him in tow? Or was she about to tell him more of the truth? 'Who to? What happened?'

Still she wanted to hold on to her secret, Tom could tell: she kept looking this way and that, her fingers agitating at the small silver bird on its chain around her neck.

'This man. Harry. I tell you he is not my father, but he goes with Matka, my mother... He brings us in England.'

'You said. So what happened? What bad thing did you do?'

'Kill him. Try to kill him – with knife.'

''Strewth!' Something moved in the straw but right now Tom couldn't take his eyes off this girl with the sudden, scared face. 'Don't tell me any more! Best if you don't. Then no one can torture it out of me!' However hard the man had been she should have gone to the police, not taken a knife to him. Except, how could an illegal immigrant do that?

'This man, he is beast,' the girl said. She shuddered. 'Matka, my mother, she is dead; he kill her!'

'What?' God! The man had killed the mother, and the girl had gone for him with a knife and run – so there had to be a woman's body lying somewhere in a blood-spattered room...

'He want me back.'

'I bet he does!'

'He has to find me. So, you help me, yes?'

'Fine. Sure. Yes. Said I would...' But there was so

much for Tom to get his head round now. The girl had attacked the man for killing her mother – and he wanted her back to shut her up. Because no one else would know – they were illegal immigrants.

'You think I run for nothing?' She smacked her own forehead, looked at him with contempt.

''Course not. But it's all down to what he knows. If he doesn't know you jumped in the sea, it won't matter that you came out. He might think you got away; or he might think you're on the run to Scotland or somewhere. If he did what he did to your mum he might think you've gone to the police, never mind what happens to you! He might be more scared than you, waiting for a knock on the door; or he might be running off himself, taking his truck abroad...'

'What? What he does to Matka?' Danni was frowning at him.

'What you said.' Tom didn't know how to repeat this – there was no easy way of slipping murder into smooth words. He came out with it, straight. 'He murdered her, didn't he?'

Suddenly Danni screeched like a stroppy kid at a teacher who wasn't funny; one shriek, short and scornful. 'What?' she burst. 'Not murder, he kill.' And she suddenly stilled. 'Matka, she die from too hard work.'

'Die? She just...died?' Which in itself wasn't a

pleasant thought, Tom didn't want it to sound all OK, but there was a world of difference between someone just dying and being murdered.

'You say "TB". This is what doctor says. But I know also, too hard work.'

So what else was Tom getting wrong about this girl?

'What did you do to him? How did you—' Not an easy question to ask.

'Knife. I stab.' The girl mimed the two-handed bringing down of a blade. Her face was suddenly as fierce as any killer.

'So why – if it wasn't for what he'd done to your mum?'

Now her eyes were staring again and she grabbed at his wrist with a fierce, shaking hand. Tom flinched. He didn't know her at all – this could end in a fit; or a stab at him with a hoofpick; or a long scream from her to be heard the other side of the church, enough to bring the vicar running. Already the dogs were snuffling outside as if they knew something was wrong.

'Matka, she die –' Danni spat out the words '– and now Danni is slave!' She poked a finger at her own chest, must have hurt herself.

'He's a bully?' Tom asked. The man must have been treating her rough – perhaps those were the bruises on her arms.

Danni kicked the straw. 'This Harry, he is like grand duke. The sister, this woman does nothing!' She clenched her fist to show his power, and Tom could see how shiny her eyes were with brooking tears. 'Everyone thinks Polski women we are slaves.'

Tom nodded as if he knew, gently, putting his arm round her shoulder, and this time there was no 'Srać!', this time she didn't shake him off. He wanted to hug her closer, to cuddle. Any thought of which flew from Tom's head as the dogs outside suddenly started barking wildly, running off from the stable door towards the gate in a high old state of excitement. Someone was coming!

'Keep down!' Tom said, jumping away from the girl. He went to the crack of the door, but he couldn't see the gate from there, so he inched out of the building and crept to the end of the outhouse to look cautiously around the corner – where Emma Thorpe was scooting her bike fast towards him, her faithful dogs running to her. Too late! She'd seen him – and his heart sank anchor deep.

CHAPTER SIX

'Tom!' She stopped. 'What in the devil's name are you doing here?'

I've got a girl in the tack room! The dogs ran on to Tom, yapping around his legs – thank God they couldn't talk! But what *did* he say? Emma was looking at him straight, this was no head-on-one-side casual enquiry. She was hot from riding her bike which gave her a ruddy, outraged look; and he was trespassing on her land.

'It was the dogs. Petra and Barney, yelping like crazy, I heard them from the other side of the church. I knew you were all out so I came to check.' Now he was in deeper, definitely lying. Which meant that Danni just did not have to be seen because nothing he said to Emma would ever be believed from now on.

'And?' Now Emma's head did go to one side.

'What?'

'Anything?'

'Oh. No.' Tom started walking away from the hot

spot, talking over his shoulder as artificially as an actor on the church-hall stage. 'I checked the stable and the...place next door...and it's all secure. Everything shipshape.'

'Good. Thanks.' But Emma was walking her bike on towards the tack room – where she kept it!

'Here, I'll park up for you...' Tom grabbed at the handlebars, praying to God that Danni didn't say something when he went in.

'Why have you come back?' he asked. Because – why *had* Emma suddenly turned up; she was on a day out with Philip Swain, wasn't she? Tom opened the tack room door, pushed the bike in quickly, and shut it.

But Emma had stopped, thank God, she wasn't coming any closer, it was only the stupid dogs still sniffing round the door.

'I didn't want to waste a whole day there,' she said. As simple as that. She was staring at Tom – and even in his ruffled state he wondered what else she was saying to him. *Tom hadn't gone with her so she hadn't stayed.* Was she saying that? *It wasn't the same with Philip Swain.* 'What about you?' she went on, quickly. 'Your little sailing friend? Did he blow you out? Or *she*?'

'That's about it,' Tom said. 'These holiday people! Kid says one thing but his dad says they're doing something else... *His* dad.' He tried a desperate twinkle.

'Ah.'

Meanwhile, how was he going to get Danni out of that tack room?

At that moment the church bell started to ring for Morning Service.

Diversion! 'The bells! Got to go.'

'You? To church?'

'Mum said she might go. I'll look to Sally.' Tom really couldn't do any better than that. And he just had to hope that Emma would clear off and get herself a drink after her hot ride. A few minutes were all a girl like Danni would need to make a run for it.

Emma looked at him the way she looked when he joked to cover up his reading and writing. Weird boy!

But Tom was on a roll, thinking. Because the church bell had just told him something else. On Sundays when the church was in use, the church hall wasn't. It was locked, secure – and who had a key? The cleaner. His mum. He and Danni could hide out in there till the time for the bus.

'Off you go, then,' Emma said.

'Yup.' Tom turned towards the gate, but somehow he had to get a message to Danni. Now, thank God, Emma came away from the outhouses and hitched her door key from her dungaree pocket.

'Hang on! My penknife!' Tom suddenly turned and ran fast to the tack room, like a playground kid in some fantasy game of his own. He pushed the dogs aside and rushed in, even pretended to look in the corner for a knife he didn't have. 'Take your chance to get out!' he hissed at Danni, hidden by a horse blanket. 'Get away! Meet me back of the church, somewhere, anywhere...' He rushed out again and ran past Emma to the gate he'd left open. 'Cheers! Got it!' he called, and patted at his empty pocket.

Emma folded her arms and shook her head. 'Poor old Tom,' she said. 'Imagine – a whole day out with you!' And she snorted as she went for the door of the house.

On which depressing note Tom ran off, alone – to walk into the ritual of the full English breakfast back at home. Fried egg, bacon, sausage, mushrooms, baked beans and tomatoes. The works. Tom's mum slaved away in the kitchen to make it perfect; and if she broke the yolk of a fried egg she ate it herself, while her husband sat at the head of the table like Lord Muck. Such was the man.

George Welton was tall and broad, and in his operational yellow oilskins he looked huge. His head was balding and he shaved himself shining smooth; he kept his nails clipped short and he demanded a twice weekly neck shave from his wife; so Tom had to have very regular haircuts, and if ever he said he was going to grow a beard he'd have been buried at sea.

Tom walked into the domestic scene, Sally in her pyjamas being fed toast fingers dipped into her father's yolk like a toddler. The man hardly looked up, but Tom got a 'Morning!' from his mother in the kitchen.

'Morning!' back.

Tom sat at the table. He was hungry; at least, he put the feeling inside down to hunger – but it could have been frustration, fright and jealousy all jumbled up together.

'Washed your hands, lad?'

'Good point,' Tom said. 'On account of I've just taken them out of a bucket of cow dung I keep down the cess pit.'

'Ha!' Tom's dad gave his view on teenage humour.

Tom went to the kitchen sink.

'Do you want a cooked breakfast, Tom?'

Tom smiled at his mum. 'No, just a quick bit of toast, thanks. Got a lot on.' And he couldn't stop his eyes going to the church-hall key on its hook by the back door.

'Toast is on the table,' his father called. 'Cold, mind, you're late.'

'Good – I like it cold. Prefer it. Did you know cold is the new hot?'

'Hmmph!'

'Saw Charlie Gull,' Tom said, going back in to sit at the table opposite his father, who was mopping up his plate. Well, his father would soon enough find out.

'We all see Charlie Gull, and Charlie Gull sees all!' his father said with what could have been an extra edge of meaning; he could well have been told of the beach hut kiss by now. Tom shot a look at him but the man didn't bother to meet Tom's eye as he went on wiping.

'He told me that girl's been seen alive.'

Now the wiping stopped. 'You could've said, boy.'

'I just did.'

'I've hurried my meal to get to the news on that.'

Tom looked at his father's plate. Hurried? Emma's dogs couldn't have made a more thorough job of shining it. 'Anyhow, she was seen by a bloke with binoculars: or *a* girl was,' he added quickly. 'Landed in a dinghy, or something.'

'Huh!' Tom's father stared at him. 'We know what that's about, then, don't we? It's some set-up job by our ethnic friends. Jump overboard and get picked up where the radar doesn't work. Worth the risk for an easy way into the soft UK...'

'How come,' Tom asked, 'if the ship was going out?'

A big hand rocked a shiny plate. 'Who said she was going out?'

'Thought you did.'

'Then you thought wrong, boy. I never said nothing about the ship – don't know about her myself. But that's typical: you have to look at it from their side, not ours. God, education…'

'Yeah,' Tom said, 'education! Tell me about it!' He put on a huff, hoped he was making a smokescreen by puffing up his own problem. But, shit, it was Danni who'd told him which way the ship was heading, not his father. And thinking of her, Tom had to be out of here, quick, with that key. If she was huddled down behind some gravestone right now she could be seen by anyone coming out of church. But his mother came in with fresh hot toast and a fried egg on top.

'Hot. Get this inside you.'

'I'll give it a home.'

'I'm going up the Coastguard,' his father was saying, 'see what we've got. Then I'll see you down at the chalet.' And, surprise, surprise, and why should he say it, suddenly coming over all human? 'Get ourselves a sail out in *Sandpiper*, eh?' He came back to the table and dipped a corner of toast into Tom's yolk and ate it – a liberty that would normally have given Tom a lift.

'Yeah, could do. Though I might be tied up a bit with some mates…'

'Oh well, please yourself.' The man got up and went to the door, searched his pockets for a small Hamlet to smoke on his off-duty walk up to the coastguard station.

Tom took his chance. Sally had cleared off, his mother was skivvying round the dining table picking up the breakfast plates; his dad had gone out. And the church-hall key was hanging there on its hook by the back door pulling him like a neon zapper attracts a fly. From where he was standing at the sink it was just a quick lean and a grab and the key was in Tom's hand.

'What are you doing?' God, his mother skivvied fast.

'Doing? What?'

'At the sink. I'm sorting this lot if you've got things on. You get off. Lowestof, is it for that new compass?'

'Oh, yeah. Could be.' He'd lost one overboard last week.

'I'll get that Sally to help me. She don't do much.'

'No, she don't.' And Tom didn't need telling twice. With a quick kiss for his surprised mother he was out of the back door and running for the church, the key still held in his hand, along the line of cottages and cutting across the corner of a beet field to bring himself out behind the church. Had Danni managed to sneak out of the tack room? Would she be somewhere here? Tom couldn't see her, and with people in the church he couldn't start calling out, but running like a kid playing Sea Kings he searched behind every tombstone, scoured under every shrub and even poked his head inside the west porch; there wasn't a mound of grass, a line of brick or a run of wall that he didn't check. But there was no sign at all of the girl; so what had gone wrong? Was she still holed up in Emma's tack room looking for a chance to make a break for it? Or had she got out and was lying low some other place – or had she taken off for Lowestoft on her own – walking, like she'd wanted?

Or had she been found by Emma and they could ground the Sea King?

Well, there was only one thing to do – Tom had to go back to Emma Thorpe's to find out.

Or, did he?

Tom stopped, drew breath, had a think. Did he have to backtrack, couldn't he just move on? He crouched hiding behind an overgrown tombstone as things started to come into focus. Should he be skulking here or were there other things he'd rather be doing, like going out in *Sandpiper* with his dad?

Hadn't he done his best for the Polish girl – who surely to God could have made a run for it by now? Wasn't he just some sort of sucker?

He stood again, stretched his aching muscles, sat on the edging of the grave and tried to puzzle it out – because what Tom Robinson Welton did next was going to be crucial. Did he go on or did he go back? The girl hadn't shown; now he'd got the chance to make the break. He could turn around, go down to the beach and his boat; or he could go on looking for Danni. He could be the Tom who'd woken up yesterday morning or the Tom who'd just nicked the church-hall key off his mother. And as he stared at a grave and idly read the name and the fading dates of someone whose life was all done and dusted, he boiled it down to one crucial question. Where would he most like to be in his best dreams? What sort of thing would he be doing if it were only down to him, with all his options open? Up to yesterday he would have chosen desert island surf rolling over and over with Emma Thorpe; Adam and Eve in their private world – him and her and no books, no writing. But as he called it up that old dream seemed clouded now, it was in a hazy mix with something else – and this other thing wasn't a fantasy at all but something real, something that had happened, a memory, an *experience*. It was the taste and the feel of being kissed by Danni, the Polish girl.

And, Je-sus, that had been something! Yes, he'd had pecks at girls, he'd played Kiss Chase and Murder in the Dark and Postman's Knock, but they'd all been at a kids' level; a thrill of an experience – not! And when he'd kissed Emma Thorpe at that party she'd been more interested in winning a prize for holding her breath than in being pressed against the Welton lips. But, Danni's kiss, that had been something else – something definitely grown up. It had been thrust at him hard, but turning gentle as her lips opened just a bit in the push of it and he'd felt her warm breath; and her body had been pressed against him, her breasts, and down there, and her knees. And all that for *show,* for Charlie Gull? Or had she meant it?

And suddenly his mind was made up. Stuff like that didn't happen every day: it didn't happen *ever!* And if it had been for the reason she'd said, didn't that mean something, too, pretending to be friends? Didn't that mean she needed him? He chewed on that. *Someone needed him?* A no-hoper? Well, that was a first! He took in a breath, swelled his chest; and he decided. He'd go back – at least take one more step.

And just hope it wasn't off some cliff.

CHAPTER SEVEN

At the manor house the dogs barked and Emma came running.

'Tom? Again? What do you want now?'

He'd had time to think this one out. 'Oh, I'm a dozo, you know I dropped my knife...?'

'So you said...'

She was suspicious, Tom knew that look. 'Yeah, well, anyhow, I think I pulled out some money, too. A couple of coins.'

'Oh.' Not convinced. 'Then you'd better check, hadn't you?'

'OK, cheers, only – a few quid's a few quid...'

'Oh yes.' She was staring him out but Tom didn't stay to dwell longer; he ran around the side of the house to the tack room and went in. But it was empty of Danni: there was no sign of her. He came out and checked in Molly's stable, too.

And suddenly Emma was in the doorway behind him. 'Got it?' she asked.

'Yeah, thanks. In here.' He jingled his mother's church-hall key against some other coins in his pocket.

'Well, all's well that ends well, I suppose,' Emma said.

'Yeah.' And with a final pat of the dogs' heads Tom walked off, not looking back because he knew what he'd see on Emma's face – some sort of pity, and he didn't want to have to carry that, he really didn't.

Danni still wasn't in the church grounds, nor in the nearest copse, nor under the tall hedgerows round the beet fields. Which meant she had to have headed for Lowestoft on her own; because that other possibility – her being found by Emma and turned in to the authorities – that couldn't have happened or Emma would have said, wouldn't she? She'd have been full of it – and linking him in, too. So Tom went home to return the church-hall key before it was missed.

And as he came from the kitchen back into the garden he suddenly stopped short – because hanging on the empty washing line was something special: the red napkin from *Beaufort* that Danni had been wearing as a headscarf. A flag: a 'red duster' as clear as the air it hung in to signal to him that the girl *was* still around. Brilliant! It lifted Tom like an ocean swell.

So, where was she? Well, she wasn't in the house –

that was all locked up with everyone down at the beach – which only left the sheds. But his dad's shed was locked, too, so he ran on to his own at the bottom of the garden. And straight off, he knew that she was in there. OK, everything said she would be; but there was something else, a knowing, a sort of vibration, a wavelength; he sensed the feel of her almost as strong as a touch.

Cautiously, he tapped the V for victory, turned the handle and opened the shed door. And as his eyes acclimatised after the glare of so much Suffolk sky, he saw her standing staring at him from the corner.

'She feeds dogs so I run!'

'You weren't up behind the church.'

Danni turned away and looked out of the little window, very much in charge of herself. 'Road too near. Harry has car…'

Tom looked round the small space, out through the grey window nets with her, into the garden, back at the house. 'So how did you know to come here?'

She shrugged. 'Where you live, you point it to me – when we go first to the stable.' As simple as that.

'Good for you!'

And it could have been nerves but her stomach suddenly rumbled.

'Srać! I am sorry.'

Of course, she was hungry – and only now he

realised like a rap on the head that he hadn't got the food with him. It wasn't a fictitious knife or coins that he'd left in Emma Thorpe's tack room but the real bag of bits and pieces! Philip Swain was right – he *was* a dozo. 'I'll get you something,' he said.

'*Dziękuję.*' Which he guessed had to be 'thank you' as she sat down on a small crate.

Tom ran to the house and found biscuits and a bottle of cola: at this rate their larder would be as empty as Old Mother Hubbard's. But so be it. Tom hurried back down the garden.

'It's still too soon to go for the bus,' he said as Danni ate and drank. 'But we can't stay here.'

'No – we can go,' Danni said around biscuit crumbs and through a burp. 'We go to Lowestoft.'

'We can't walk it.'

She grabbed his hand, took him to the shed door. 'We go like this,' she said – and led him around the back. The hand holding he liked; but what he saw he didn't; he didn't like it at all. It was a bike, a Wingrave 300-X.

'Where'd you get this?' But he knew very well where she'd got it – from where Emma Thorpe would pretty soon miss it.

'It is there. I take. You take back after.'

'Yeah, I'll take back.' The words came out of his brain-dead head; it was as if he was out in *Sandpiper* and he'd suddenly lost his tiller. Being with this girl was like sailing where you'd never sailed before. But there was cheek and dare on her face – and how could anyone not go along with eyes that shone at you like that, and a mouth that suddenly smiled like a sea flower opening? Of course he could get Emma's bike back to her, no prob, he'd leave his own locked up in Lowestoft, go back for it after, and tell Emma he'd found hers somewhere, there must have been a prowler like he'd thought. Anything.

Meanwhile his own Raleigh was right here in the shed.

But there was a nagging. 'Why didn't you just go, on her bike? Why come here?'

The girl stared at him, her eyes narrowing, her mouth pursing. 'You don't want?'

'Yeah, I do want. I'm just asking, because you were all for going on your own before.'

She kept up the staring at him, and she shrugged again. 'Perhaps, I like Tom.' She said it straight, no smile on her mouth but her eyes twinkled just a bit. 'Perhaps you say the truth. Two look better than one.' And the distant rattle of the Sea King came in on cue to bear out her words. Except, Tom preferred the first explanation.

Back inside the shed Danni put her hand on his saddle. 'We go, uh?'

'Yeah, OK, we go. But you promise me something, will you?'

'What? What, I promise you?'

'If the Sea King, that helicopter…if it goes over while we're on the road you don't panic and dive in a ditch or anything. They'll see you and they'll know.' Now she was pouting, he'd offended her; but he went on. 'I'll wave to them like the trippers do and you hold steady.'

Danni stared him in the eyes again. 'I do not panic. But I wave, same as you,' she said slowly.

'Great. Because you'll be OK being with me…'

'No, I will wave because I wave goodbye England, I have to go from that Harry. This is why I will wave.'

'Yeah, 'course it is.' And put firmly in his place now, Tom found his bicycle padlock and wheeled the Raleigh out of the shed. 'Right, pal,' he said, defiantly pulling up her hood again. 'Off to jolly Lowestoft.'

It was single file north. From the top of the town where Tom lived, the route to Lowestoft took them straight out along narrow B roads where a tractor and load could hold up even a cyclist. But early that Sunday afternoon it was easy going. The sun was still warm with a few clouds forming although Tom's only interest in the sky was the possibility of the Sea King coming over. He hadn't heard it for a while now, but like the jet fighters from RAF Wattisham he knew it could suddenly roar across the flat landscape as if it had burst up from out of a hole.

It was about ten miles to Lowestoft but they couldn't stick to B roads all the way. At Wrentham they'd have to join the A12 and then the ride would change; instead of the odd car giving them a wide berth there'd be a stream of vehicles rocking their balance with their slipstreams. But the first bit was pleasant; warm, quiet, boy and girl out for a ride. Tom looked around at Danni following and she took a hand off her handlebar to wave at him. Her hood had fallen back, she was in the red headscarf again, she'd rolled up her sleeves and her arms were shining tanned in the sun. And Tom's stomach turned with a sudden sense of loss. Wouldn't this have felt good if it wasn't for what the end would bring – him cycling back home along this road alone? Because now he knew he'd miss her. He looked around at her again and she wobbled, and he wobbled, too; on his bike for a joke, and inside for real. How could he ever have been in two minds in the churchyard?

The final stretch of the A12 into Lowestoft itself is long and straight and on this busy summer Sunday it was packed. Tom and Danni had to weave their bikes in and out of traffic, walk them across lights, and sometimes use the pavement. In the town Danni had suddenly changed; she took over the lead; her hood was up again, her face was tense and her eyes were everywhere – and Tom's were, too, although he hadn't got any idea who they were looking for, he hadn't thought to ask for a description beyond the trucker looking like a fish. He reckoned his first alert would be a scream. She led them along the London road into Station Square where she got off Emma's bike and pushed it into a parking slot in the paving outside Lowestoft Central railway station. Tom put his bike next to hers and chained them in a pair.

What now? his face asked, but he only had to follow to know. Through the throng of holidaymakers she led him up the main shopping precinct and turned them left along a side street into a long road with houses on one side and the railway line on the other. They could have come into this road direct, but she'd deliberately brought him the long way round through the crowds.

'Here, I live,' she said. 'Denmark Road.' And she pointed along to the far end, pulling her hood tighter. 'And Harry and his sister.'

Tom looked up and down the road, which was empty. 'Come a bit close, haven't we?'

'Must. The ships, they are over there.' Danni pointed beyond the railway line. 'What ships are here, is very important... What is ready for going...'

But they were still walking towards the dangerous Harry end of the road. Did they have to go past his house to get around to the docks? Then Danni stopped. 'I do not want ship with Harry in it!'

'No, you don't – but it's got to be going to Poland. How will you know?'

'The name; the flag.'

'And what about him?'

'His ships I know. They have the yellow lorries.'

'But it could be someone else?'

She nodded. 'Six lorries, six drivers. We watch, we see, I don't go in any ship.'

She was right, of course. She'd been dead lucky to survive once; to find she was on a ship with Harry and jump overboard again would be asking for a miracle. Her eyes were still everywhere – Tom keeping pace with her, desperate to know what house was Harry's but not daring to ask – when without any warning Danni suddenly ran across the road onto the other pavement, on the railway side. In a gap in the fence she pushed at a railing gate and Tom could see why. The gate led onto a long footbridge across eight or ten railway lines over to the docks.

She led the way like a fairground girl leading a boy off into the woods. Her hood was up but her back was straight, she had a purpose and a swagger to her walk. And Tom followed. But it was exposed up on the footbridge, just an open lattice of metal struts. Crossing it, they would be seen from both sides as well as from below – and it was a long way across. From up here Tom could see over to the quayside of the docks with the security and weighbridge buildings and several smallish freight ships moored alongside in a line. They walked fast but still no one was in sight, the girl staring at the container ships.

'The names, I see them...' She was squinting at the nearest. The ship had 'Sea Crest' painted on it, over an old metal outline of another name, something else she'd been before. They changed owners, they changed names: unlike the few fishing vessels across the harbour which were identified by numbers and letters – the same as *Sandpiper*, Tom's 14414. And his stomach flipped at the thought that the man with the binoculars from beach hut thirty-three might have made a note of it when he'd seen him rescue Danni. Tom Robinson Welton could still have all that to face...

'What?'

Danni had stifled a cry and stopped. Tom looked down where her eyes led him, to the third ship in the line – which had a yellow lorry and trailer on it.

'Harry – could be!' Danni hissed. 'Could not be; we see the lorry number.' She was looking hard and so was Tom but they'd have to get a lot closer to read it.

She crouched and made her way forward. There was activity on the ship and from the way the deck was fully loaded she couldn't be long off sailing. But anyone might look up and see them now, stalking across the bridge towards the quay. With her hood up Danni looked like any kid up to no good.

There didn't seem to be any actual security about, though. The dock gate was non-existent, the weighbridge building was shut up, the security portacabin had a faded picture of an Alsation on it but there were no guards inside – and this footbridge over the railway led directly down to the quayside from which anyone could walk onto a ship. Right now a couple of seamen were coming to the quay from the town carrying plastic Somerfield bags.

'I'll go,' said Tom. 'No one knows me, I could be crew. I'll get the licence number and come back.'

But Danni had stopped. She held Tom with a fierce grip. A railwayman in an orange bib had come from the track beneath and was heading for the footbridge steps, up towards them from the dock side. And he was frowning at them. Were they trespassing on railway property? They could be the sort of vandals who threw stuff onto the tracks, they could be taggers with aerosol cans in their pockets.

Tom was taking no chances. 'Get back over in the street,' he said. 'Walk casual; we'll come back later.'

As one, they turned and faced back across the footbridge. To see a tallish man with a limp coming from the other direction, oiled silver hair, looked about sixty, a Boss bag over his shoulder.

And Danni suddenly screamed. 'Srać!' she yelled. 'Srać!' And from the look of terror on her face Tom knew without doubt that this man coming towards them was the Harry she was running from.

CHAPTER EIGHT

The man started coming faster despite the limp.

'Dan-*u*ta!' he shouted and broke into a hobbling run.

Tom swore. Panicked, he looked all around. This bullying Harry was coming one way, the railwayman the other – and he and Danni were trapped between them with the rails a death jump below.

'God, girl!'

But Danni knew what to do. She ran hard for the railwayman pulling down her hood and whipping off her headscarf. She shook her head, flashed her curling black hair, showed him she was a girl.

'Please!' she shouted at him. 'Monster! This man is monster!'

The trucker was running at them shouting. 'Dan-*u*ta! Stop will you? Come here! I'm not going to…!'

'No, stop *him*!' Tom picked up on Danni's shouts as he ran after her. The railwayman was frowning, shot a look at them, a look at the trucker, looked like he didn't know what to do – till he beefed himself up to let Danni through, then Tom, and stood solid in the path of Harry.

'What's all this, then, mate?'

'Let me through, you don't know nothing!' Harry shouted.

'Hang on, boy, you sure what you're doing?' the railwayman said – balking the trucker enough to hold him up while Tom and Danni ran for the footbridge steps.

'Get out of it! That's my stupid daughter! Danni, come back here!' Harry pushed past the railwayman and clattered at the top of the steps; but Tom and Danni were younger and they'd taken them three at a time to get down to the quay; had the start on him that they needed. They ran out of the docks like fugitives, along the empty industrial road back towards the railway station. Harry came limping on fast, Tom could see him a hundred metres back before turning the last corner – and with the fastest sailors' fingers he'd ever used, he unlocked the bikes for them to scoot off fast along Marine Parade.

Head down on the road to Somerthorpe, every car coming past was a threat until it had gone safely on, although Tom reckoned the man wouldn't know Danni had got a bike and he'd probably be scouring Lowestoft right now. They pedalled fast, Danni leading, no time for words. *What a stroke she'd pulled!* Tom thought. Himself, he'd frozen, had no idea of what to do except butt the railwayman in the stomach to let Danni get away – but that was his thinking now. She'd done the business, though, quick action. She'd shown the man she was a girl and they'd got away with it.

Which was what she'd done with Charlie Gull and the kiss at the beach hut. So was that how she got around threatening men? Using her sex? Was that what life as a girl illegal immigrant had taught her to do?

And that Harry! *He was an old man.* Tom had seen him as a great hulking trucker, thick as a beet labourer, but he was more like a granddad. No, Tom reckoned as he pedalled on fast, the unpleasant people in life never quite look the way we think. But he could certainly see the sort of creepy bully the trucker had to be.

They left Emma's bike hidden in bushes up behind the church hall where Tom could pretend to find it later – there *had* been someone prowling, hadn't there? He came to his house on his own while Danni stayed under cover in a hedgerow. It was still early evening and he hoped the family hadn't come up from the beach; and he was lucky, the house was all locked up so he ran Danni and his bike back down to his shed.

'Nothing else for it, you'll have to stay here tonight,' he said. 'We can't risk the church hall in case they find the bike up there – they might look inside.'

'Why do I come?' It was the first thing Danni had said for ages with the push of the ride.

'To England?'

'No!' She cracked her fingers in a whippy gesture. 'To here, back.'

'To hide. To keep out of Harry's way.'

'Long way from Harry's way! Why not I hide in the town? Still I do not know if it is Harry's lorry going in Poland so I go on another ship...'

'Well, you're here now.' God, this girl was hard to please. 'Perhaps you didn't want to say goodbye to me!' Which was a chance at a joke, a light remark, but it came out sounding a million times too serious.

All the same, she turned round at him as she slipped into the shed with a lingering look, and away. 'Perhaps you are right.' And he really couldn't tell whether she was joking, too – or not.

'Anyhow, he knows you're not dead so if he's going he'll be looking till the tide's right.' And if he wasn't going, he had also seen Tom; which meant that if the local paper reported a boy rescuing a girl from the rocks in an identified dinghy Harry would know just where to come. All ends up, Danni couldn't stay here for long!

'Whatever, it's you here for tonight. Tomorrow we'll plan again.'

Without a word Danni sat herself down on the crate and started fingering the silver bird on her necklace. Her face said everything; she *had* been joking; she was disappointed as hell that she hadn't got away from England tonight.

But Tom wasn't. He liked being with this lively, unpredictable girl. 'Anyhow,' he admitted, 'on the bright side I don't have to say goodbye to you for one more day.' He felt himself blush, but she didn't look up. He changed tack quickly. 'I'll get you a blanket from the house before the others come back.' And a sudden thought. 'Do you want to use the loo? If you're quick?'

'Loo?'

'The lav? Lavatory? Toilet? Bathroom? WC? But you'd have to be quick.'

She shook her head.

Tom dwelt no further on that. But the blanket was urgent; it could be cold tonight and the family would be up from the beach at any time. 'Hang on,' he said, as if she were likely to do anything else, and he raced to the house and came back with a blanket from the top of his own wardrobe. 'You can stretch out,' he said, 'if you keep curled up!' He laughed at his own joke, but Danni didn't seem to understand it.

'*My name is De-rek and this is my cage!*' a voice suddenly sounded, impersonating something off TV. '*My name is De-rek and this is my cage!*'

Shite! Tom froze. It was Sally and she was coming down the garden path! Like a rat from a beet mound, he was out of the shed and shutting it behind him. Sally came on towards him wearing someone else's face.

'*My name is De-rek and this is my cage!*'

'Hi De-rek,' Tom said. 'Got out, old boy?' He scooped Sally up fighting, onto his back for a bucking horse ride she didn't want, around and around on the tufty grass. And with an embarrassing 'Gallopy, gallopy, gallopy!' while she tried to heel him in the groin, he trotted around the garden and up into the kitchen, where he set her down and closed the back door firmly behind him.

'You big idiot!' she said – as a knocking came at the front door. But no one they knew ever came to the front; it was so unusual that it shut Sally up.

George Welton went to see who it was. 'Yes?'

It was Philip Swain, holding a carrier bag in his hand.

'Mr Welton?'

'You've got him.'

'I think this is Tom's.'

'Well, you want Tom, then, boy, not me.'

But Tom was there already. 'Hiya Phil!' There was no question of Tom asking him in; all he wanted was to get the pain away. Because in his hand Swain was holding the plastic carrier with that morning's food for Danni. The bag he'd left at Emma's place.

'Don't know the why's and wherefore's,' Swain said, 'but this bag was in the tack room. With food in, like a picnic.'

'Oh?'

'Only Emma said you were there?' he snooted at Tom.

George Welton smiled and shot Tom a quick look. Being alone with Emma Thorpe and a picnic would be the dream of many.

'Cheers,' Tom said and took the bag.

'Don't know anything about her bike, do you?' Swain asked. 'Found it up behind the church hall...'

Now that Tom looked, Emma Thorpe's Wingrave X-300 was leaning behind Swain at the gate. 'No, she had it when I left her. And she waved me goodbye,' he added for good measure, because it was true.

But George Welton's hand had landed on his son's shoulder like plod. 'A secret feast in the hay loft?'

'Something like,' said Tom.

'Thanks,' George Welton said to Philip Swain, making to shut the door.

But Swain had a chess-master face on, not a hint of the surprise move he was about to make. 'Oh, and this was in the bag. I kept it separate, thought it might be important…' From his pocket he took out a piece of paper ruled in squares like from a French exercise book. He held it up. It was crinkled, it had been wet and folded. He read out what was written on it in ballpoint. '"*RF 303 White House/Bronislau Mikawski.*" Last bit looks like Polish to me,' he said.

Polish? The sound of Swain saying the word flooded Tom's face with guilt. As the pit of his stomach hit his throat he took the paper. *Polish!* Which meant Danni had dropped it!

'Not your dinghy, is it?' Philip Swain was going on. 'RF 303 – they have markings on their sails, don't they?'

'M14414,' Tom and his father said together.

'Or your car?'

'No.'

'Only –' Swain said; and Tom couldn't bear the wait for the rest of the sentence; ' – my holiday project's on Codes, Markings and Identifications, they've all got their own pattern and a rhyme and a reason: postcodes, bar codes, car registrations…'

'It's for *my* project, as it happens.' Tom put the paper in his pocket and took over the shutting of the door. 'Cheers.' And, 'Snobby bastard!' as he walked into the living room to an 'Oi!' from his father.

Tom had to wait half an hour for *New Pop Idols* to come on the television before he could slide out to the garden and run down to his shed. He did the V for victory knock and said, 'Tom,' going in.

Danni was sitting huddled there with the blanket around her, nothing to do, nothing to read or listen to, nothing to look at.

'You all right?'

'I breathe.'

'He wasn't what I expected,' Tom suddenly had to say. 'Harry.'

'When are they?' Danni wanted to know. She shuddered, hugged herself – and after his own fright, too, all Tom wanted to do suddenly was put his arm around this girl. She looked forlorn again, like that first time in the dinghy, she'd lost some of her spirit out here on her own, she was very close to crying. But he kept what distance he could in the small space.

'Got this,' he said. 'It was in the bag. This yours?' He didn't go into the Philip Swain visit but just handed her the squared paper.

She took it. And now she did go, now she did lose it; a sob caught her throat and within seconds she was heaving her shoulders and crying tears that came from body deep. And Tom could do nothing else now: he did put an arm round her which she pushed off at first, but together they slid to the floor, where he first wiped her tears with his fingers and then tried with the palm of his hand to still the wailing she was starting.

'Shhh! No! It's all right, I'm here. I'm your friend and I'm going to help you. Shhh! Please – they'll hear you, someone'll come…'

But she was racked now, getting louder and trying again to push him off.

'Sorry,' Tom said, coming away.

Danni looked at him. 'No, is not you,' she said, and she put a hand to his cheek. 'Is *him!*' and she shuddered.

At that moment a fox barked and a high pitched yelping started up. It was a vixen with cubs, a sound that sometimes brought George Welton to his back door with a shotgun.

'I've got to go!' Tom reached forward and wiped more tears with his fingers, which she allowed; a different kid tonight.

She put her fingers to her lips, she had quietened now, and she put the same fingers to his lips. A blessing. 'You are good friend…' she said.

'Dunno about good but I'm your friend. And I'm going to help you till you get what you want.' He lifted the little bird on its chain round her neck and kissed it, a proxy kiss, and he backed out of the shed, never wanting so much not to have to go. 'See you in the morning, Dan. God bless.'

And she nodded, and huddled back under her blanket.

Indoors, the television programme was still on. Through the crack of the door Tom saw the three of them in there, Sally ready for bed, his father behind a paper, and their mother sewing a button on a coastguard trouser while she watched.

Tom went upstairs and lay on his bed, fully clothed. He stared at the ceiling, the old familiar ceiling he'd stared at since he was a kid. He felt heavier on the bed tonight, longer, stronger, somehow; he put his hands behind his head and thought of that girl out there. Just the fact of it! Last night he'd been hiding up a girl down in the beach hut; tonight he actually had a girl out there in his shed! His world had gone crazy, no way was he the old Tom Robinson Welton any more. And what a girl! You looked at her and you heard gypsy music, saw camp fires, felt yourself running free. You were with her and your breath was always short, she was a girl you could feel without touching. But she had let him calm her crying; and wouldn't it be great if she were up here in his room with him, just so he could comfort her? But next best was to see her in his head, her black, curling hair, her mouth when she smiled, her white teeth, her big dark eyes; to feel the press of her body against him all the way down when they'd kissed at the chalet; to hear the soft growl of her voice when she'd said perhaps he was right about her not wanting to say goodbye to him...

And in his trance world, his real ears failed him. He didn't hear his father coming up the stairs; he didn't hear him get to the bedroom door and push it open. But he saw him chuck his head and smile.

'Emma Thorpe?' he asked. 'Sweet dreams!'

Tom jumped up and smoothed the duvet. God, what a rumpled world it was!

CHAPTER NINE

Early on the Monday morning, two people were off about their business. One was George Welton who was walking from the cottage up to the coastguard station on Bleak Point. The other was Emma Thorpe who was exercising Molly. The weather was still bright, although a slight breeze coming off the sea warned that Somerthorpe might have had the best of its summer. The east coast of Britain isn't the Mediterranean, and while its sunshine record is good, lying on beaches and floating in unchilled waters had been a rare holidaymakers' treat for the past few days. *Brisk* was the word for most Somerthorpe activities, and right now brisk was how George Welton was walking and Emma Thorpe was riding.

She had her hard hat on, as well as her body protector under a summer jumper; and today on the horse it was jeans and boots instead of bare legs and shorts. Her expression was tight, chin up and shrink-wrapped, the way people in charge of big animals hold their faces; but if she wasn't looking as drop-dead gorgeous as she had to Tom two nights before, she still brought a smile to George Welton's polished face.

''Morning, young lady,' he seemed to have to say, with a crackly wave of his waterproof.

''Morning,' said Emma, her eyes glancing away from the horizon for a second.

'He's still asleep,' the coastguard said, 'having his sweet dreams!'

Instead of a reply Emma Thorpe kicked Molly and cantered off. George Welton strode on himself towards the sea, his face set hard to disguise a little whistle of an old tune.

But Tom wasn't asleep and he wasn't dreaming. As soon as his father was out of the house he came out of his room and went for a quick check on Danni. Avoiding his mother in the bathroom, he took a can of cola and a packet of Jaffa cakes down the garden to the shed. He gave his knock and Danni opened up.

'Come! Come! Hurry!'

'I came as quick as I could.' But Tom guessed it must have seemed like midday to the girl instead of seven-thirty.

She made a disbelieving little cluck in her throat, the sort of sound most English can't make. But she wasn't frowning. She looked fresher, she must have slept OK, and he could see that already she'd been out. Her hair and trainers were still wet. 'Cold!' she said, pointing to the crop spray over in the beet field. He pictured her showering naked under it, the way she'd been on the rocks, and he had to dive straight in with his plan.

'You got a watch?' No, she hadn't, stupid question – her only jewellery was the chain round her neck with the flying bird on it; she had no rings, no visible studs, no earrings. 'Give us an hour and a half. Mum goes to clean the church hall and she'll take Sally. I've got to sweep out the boat and bash the books. Then I'm yours.'

'Too long!'

'Well, we've got to be safe, that's all I can say.' He turned to go; well, if she didn't want his help...

'You can say hello.' She was staring at him; and now she leant towards him and kissed him softly on the lips. And he stayed.

'Right. I'll tell you what's happening.' With the kiss still on his lips he heard his own voice as if it were someone else's. 'We'll get you off to the church hall as soon as Mum's out of it – hide you up till we go for a ship later.'

'All the day!'

'Which is why you've got to be more comfortable than this. And safer. If he finds out it was my dinghy he could come here...'

'Sraċ!' she spat out.

'You eat those Jaffa cakes and I'll be back before you know it, OK?'

She shrugged and sat back on the crate.

'You know I'm your man.' He felt suddenly emboldened by being alone with her in his own shed, and by the kiss. 'I won't muck you about.'

'No. This I think.' Danni fixed his eyes with a look that said there was no way she'd allow being mucked about. With a quick wave and his eyes all round for nosy Sally, Tom went, running off down towards the beach.

To be suddenly brought up short as he came to *Beaufort*. Like a patrol that had timed its arrival to coincide with Tom's, Charlie Gull and a female police officer were walking briskly along from the Seal Bay direction.

'Ah!' said Charlie, arranging and rearranging the belts and buckles of his official machines. 'The very man.'

Tom looked behind him: not seriously, but wasn't that what jaunty people did for a laugh? 'Oh, me!' And he smiled. 'Has my deck chair time run out?'

'Too early,' said Charlie Gull with the sense of humour of a yak.

'Just come from Seal Bay,' said the police officer. 'There yesterday, weren't you?' She was short and lifted herself onto her toes to punctuate her words.

'No,' said Tom. 'Saturday. My dad could've been there yesterday, I think he went out in the dinghy.'

'Meant Saturday,' the woman corrected. 'Sorry.'

But she wasn't. Tom looked hard at her as she flicked the pages of a notebook. She was stocky with a big bosom – and very much the boss.

'Missing girl,' she said, 'seen in a Mirror dinghy on Saturday.'

'Yeah, I know about her,' Tom said quickly. 'Charlie and my dad told me. My dad's a coastguard, he had to work late. She was in the sea off a ship and got picked up somewhere... Didn't she?'

Charlie Gull sniffed, growled in his throat; non-verbal for his opinion of whatever immigrant scam was going on.

'Think they headed for Seal Bay,' the police officer said. 'There on Saturday, you say? You?'

Did she have a look in her eye that said she was on to him? 'I was everywhere on Saturday.' Tom knew it was always convincing to lie through telling part of the truth; he did it all the time in school – and he had to head her off. He looked around, lowered his voice, came back to the pair of them as Charlie Gull moved his head closer. 'Had this big row at home. Swore at my mum. Badly. Went sailing to chill out. Then I thought my dad might see me so I beached in Seal

Bay. I'm not supposed to sea-sail on my own with the shipping lane so close an' all...' And he wasn't supposed to be harbouring an illegal immigrant. Tom Robinson Welton was risking a lot, was in really deep water right now.

'Any other Mirrors there?'

'Not when I was. Tons around though.' He waved an arm at the sea. 'More Mirrors than a glass shop.'

But Charlie Gull was making his throat and leather noises. 'I'll say you was everywhere, Saturday. You was kissing a girl right here.'

'So?'

Charlie Gull breathed in deeply. 'Some kiss for the open promenade, you ask me.'

'I'm not asking you.'

The police officer still had her notebook open. 'Don't suppose you'd care to give us this girl's name?' she asked, more a demand.

'Don't suppose I would,' said Tom.

'Don't suppose he knows!' huffed Charlie Gull.

But while he was putting on his rebel act of denying them, Tom was nagging at something *he* wanted to know – although he hardly dared to ask. He turned to Charlie Gull, got as far as opening his mouth. He wanted to know if binocular man had remembered the number on the dinghy's sail, that would tell him how deep the water was that he was in. And he shut his mouth again as he suddenly realised that if they did know that number, this pair would have been asking him to show them his dinghy, unfurl his sail. If that number was in her notebook, she'd have nailed Tom Robinson Welton already, got his name from the Mirror sales register. So they didn't know – and he kept quiet, just.

'Some sort of girlfriend, then, was she?' the police officer asked.

Tom looked at the ground. And then he played his ace. He took the woman's arm and eased her away from Charlie Gull. 'My dad knows my girlfriend,' he said, 'he can tell you her name, she's a friend of the family.' A slight pause for effect. 'But that wasn't who Charlie saw me with. It was a holiday girl staying here. And I don't want...' He made some moves with his hands that he'd picked up from Charlie Gull sorting his straps and equipment; awkward, complicated, tangled.

'Bit of a laddo, are you, then?' the police officer said.

'Don't know about that...' Tom smiled. And he knew that he'd just done all right for himself.

'Finished here.' The woman brought Charlie Gull into things again. 'See what reports we've had from Search and Rescue and the road patrol boys...'

'Could be the immigrant mafia and she's one of the

flood,' Charlie Gull said. 'That's what I told the *Echo* and the radio.'

Which Tom knew he had to try to nail, straight off. The less explosive illegal immigrant talk banging around the better: who wanted a local witch hunt with Danni still around? 'How come?' he asked. 'My dad said the ship was going out. What's the scam if this girl's not coming in?'

The police officer held him with his eyes. He'd done it again! He'd said too much, he'd got her wondering. Why would he give a toss this holiday Monday morning?

'Take cough medicine, these people, swig drugs to make them drowsy, keeps the kids from kicking up in the lorries. Found the bottles in lifeboats, rope lockers, holds, in with the plastics of pee. Wherever she was hidden, our girl could have slept all through the ship turning around.'

'Yeah,' said Tom. 'Hadn't though of that. Will that be all, then?'

'Shouldn't it be?'

'Unless anyone else fancies a kiss?' The cheekiest, most daring thing Tom had ever said; but he made sure he was looking at Charlie Gull when he said it.

'Not on duty.' The police officer was unimpressed. And slapping her notebook shut she turned towards the town – and perhaps towards the coastguard station and Tom's father – with Charlie Gull following, still adjusting his straps.

Tom fished for the beach-hut key. He'd probably just about got away with it.

But the police officer suddenly stopped, and turned back. 'We're making an appeal for photographs,' she said, 'if you know of any. Holidaymakers, on the beach.'

'A competition?' Tom asked.

'Evidence. Someone must have that dinghy in the background of a snap or a video – with the number on its sail...' And before she went she gave Tom a tight little nod of her head. *Watch your back!*

Tom watched them go and then gave *Sandpiper* the quickest brush out she had ever had and ran back to the house. His mother had taken Sally to her cleaning of the church hall; but to put some credit in his bank he made it look as if he'd been working on his project. He got out his books and spread a wartime map of the area over the table, holding its corners down with a dictionary, a Thesaurus, 'The Somerthorpe Story' and a book about wartime RAF airfields. This was the one bit of local history he'd hoped he'd get his teeth into till he'd been smacked in the mouth by the stupid spelling of 'squadron'. And the map reading he liked – already he'd found the dotted lines of the old RAF runway where Watson's beet fields were today: so, like little markers, he stood folded tickets from the wartime play his mother had taken him to see in the church hall – making it look like a skilled, fascinating piece of research; pure Philip Swain stuff. It was quick, easy and showy – before he ran down the garden to Danni.

She looked good. After her early morning shower in the beet irrigation her t-shirt had dried and her little bird on its chain flew shining silver against the white. She had more colour in her cheeks, her eyes had lost their tired look, and her dark hair peeped out from the red headscarf like a gypsy dancer's.

'So, we go to good place?' she asked.

'Yup.' But first he told her about the police going to Seal Bay and then questioning him.

'For me, you are lying...'

'For you, Dan, I've been lying for two days. For you I don't mind lying. But now they know you weren't drowned – and so does Harry – so we keep you hidden till we go for the ship. And we make double sure about it...'

'Tonight!' She grabbed his arm.

'Hopefully. You give me his lorry's licence number, I'll check on the ship and on the dock first. Then off you go.' He'd prepared for goodbye yesterday; last night he'd had the bonus of the touch, this morning the kiss; but he knew he had to lose her today. Her hand was still gripping his arm and he covered it with his.

At the contact she took hers off. 'Where to, we go?' she asked.

'Didn't I say? The church hall. My mum's round there now. When she gets in from cleaning it, I nip indoors and nick the key off the hook, and when I give the signal we go there. No one uses the place much in the holidays, she's the only one who gets in there, my mum. So we go there when the coast is clear. OK?'

Danni shrugged. 'What you say.'

Tom checked the shed; they would have to leave no more clues behind like the carrier bag that Philip Swain had brought to the house.

'Oh, yeah – what was that bit of paper? With the writing on. What you put in the bag?' There was so much about this girl that he still didn't know – and he had all day.

'Belong to Matka,' she said. 'Like this,' she fingered her neck chain, 'it is all she leave.' She said it simply, no grief showing now.

'Ah. This is cool.' Tom crooked a finger into the chain, just lightly touching her neck before coming away.

'Eagle. Polish eagle.' The eagle was swooping with a little wreath in its beak.

'Looks real. Could be flying. And what's the paper?'

Danni said nothing for a moment; but her face told him she was deciding whether or not to tell him. Then, 'It says why Matka comes here in England,' she said. 'Why she wants here, not west, not north.' She flapped a hand at the rest of the world.

'What, this part?'

'We have time?' Danni asked him.

'Till Mum comes back.'

She looked out of the shed window and back at Tom before she slid to sit down. Tom went, too, their knees tight and touching. 'Matka has kiosk, Warsaw Central...'

'What's that, ice creams and sweets?'

Danni shook her head. 'Tickets for bus, cigarettes, newspapers. In railway station, under the road.'

'Ah.' It must have been a kiosk like those in the London Underground.

'But is all drugs there.'

Tom nodded. This was a scene he knew about; a load of drugs stuff went on round Somerthorpe; it went on in Joe Low's or the Beach Bum Bar but he wasn't a part of all that, he didn't even fancy a smoke. If he'd ever had the luck to go to a club with Emma Thorpe he'd have had ecstasy enough.

'They make her sell,' Danni was going on. 'She says

no, finish, enough. They hurt her. At the end she says she will go to police.' She stopped, took a deep breath, then said simply: 'Big mistake.'

'And you want to go back to *that*?'

Danni gave him a long, long look, as if she were trying to read him carefully enough to know whether or not to say more. 'Matka works in kiosk, it is all we have. I work, too. I take sandwiches to stall people, sell frocks for this one, shoes for that one... For little time Matka thinks it is finished with this gang. But, no – they come to her again. "Sell drugs, sell drugs, sell drugs."' Danni stared Tom in the face. 'But Matka is brave. She says they must kill her because she will not sell drugs!'

'*Well* brave!' Tom said. '*Well* brave!'

'But they are clever. Now it is not her; it is me.' Danni said it straight and matter-of-fact. 'Now these men, they take me.'

'No!' Tom's inside suddenly turned with a jealous curdle. Thugs taking this special girl! Harming her! 'What did they do to you?'

'Needle,' she said, doing the action of a syringe into her arm. 'They take me to Praga Park, they hold me down on the grass, they put in needle...'

Words had run out on Tom, he just stared at her. She'd had *that* done to her? Had they freaked her, made her an addict? Her story got worse and worse as she went on. Now he wanted to hug her again, tell her she was all right now. And he wanted to kiss her, achingly badly he wanted to kiss her. He pulled himself up, changed position in the tight space and leant towards her.

But somewhere outside the shed there were sudden shouts, men's voices, close by. Tom twisted fast to look through the window towards the house – no one there – he opened the door a crack as Danni shrank into the shadows.

'Ha' you got a smoke, Sam?'

'No, boy. Nor ain't got a drink, neither.'

'Never 'as, you!'

Tom could see them through the slit in the door opening. They were two labourers from the beet fields, Sam Matthews and Ted someone, trailing along the hedge on the other side of the wire boundary fence.

'Well, she ain't on our land.'

''Course she ain't.'

'Pity, that. Don' mind finding a girl as wants hiding up secret...'

'Yarrr!'

They rubbed their hands and laughed as they went on down the line of the hedge. And Tom knew what this was about. The year before, Arthur Watson who owned the land had taken on some seasonal beet lifters who'd turned out to be illegal – and he'd paid a big fine at Norwich Court, just escaped a month in prison. If there was a chance a load more had landed – if people like Charlie Gull on the radio were saying Danni could be one of a batch of illegal immigrants – he didn't want them found on his patch. So the Somerthorpe witch hunt was on!

And now the man Ted was calling across to Tom's garden.

'Oi there, little Sally. A'right?'

'Yup! Ta!'

Tom swiftly shut the shed door. His mother was back from the church hall, Sally was in the garden; but thank God the men in the field had been enough to send her indoors.

'Don't go away!' Tom told Danni. He tried to sound in control but he wasn't, he didn't know what to think. He just felt bashed around, like *Sandpiper* in a squall. 'Keep your head down!' He slid out of the shed and walked whistling up to the house: Captain Calm of the *Smooth Waters*.

Inside, his mother was looking at his table of project work. 'That's more my old Tom,' she said. 'I'm not much myself, but I'm a tryer. An' that's what you are, boy.'

'Cheers!'

'We're my side of the family,' she said, suddenly

turning to give him a fierce hug. She lowered her voice. 'Sally's Jack Flash quick. But us two, we do bloody try, don' we?'

'We do!' Tom said. 'We bloody do!'

And he would. With what he'd just heard out there in the shed he was more determined than ever that Tom Robinson Welton was never going to be faulted for trying to help an illegal immigrant.

CHAPTER TEN

He had to do it without the key, though. His mother didn't hang it up and he couldn't be sure which of her pockets it was in – not sure enough for a quick dive in and grab. And Sally was in one of her all over the place moods – she could be up in her bedroom one minute and down in the garden the next. So Tom would have to take a chance at getting into the church hall. He slid out of the back door, walked fast down the garden, and when the place seemed empty of anything but sky ran doubled over along the line of hedge, Danni out of the shed and close behind.

He reckoned he knew a way into the building. Besides, if the vicar found signs of someone being there, it wouldn't look like an inside job; key holders are always the first to be questioned. At the back of the hall there were the lavatories, Men's and Women's. The Men's had a small window with a broken catch; what should have been a long arm with holes in it for fixing the window open was a fractured stump, held shut and only looking secure; but Tom guessed it would only need a good push to force it. Coming to it he looked for something to stand on, but Danni was a jump ahead. Seeing what he was up to, she went to the wall, stood with her back to it and made a stirrup with her hands, cocking her head for him to come on.

'*Przybyć!*' she said. 'Hands, shoulders.'

'Are you sure?'

'Of course, sure!'

Quickly, one of a drilled team, he climbed into Danni's hands and up onto her shoulders to push hard at the window frame. She held fiercely onto the backs of his legs and after a couple of pushes the catch gave.

'*Dobry!*' She clicked a sort of congratulation with her teeth.

Wriggling through headfirst Tom hung down above the wash basin. It was tight and awkward, and he cracked his head on the porcelain when he had to let himself go – but at least he was in. He sorted his feet and ran out across the hall to the main door.

But it was locked, of course it was! And the key was back in his own house. Using a hall chair to climb up onto the lavatory sink, he leant out of the window and offered a hand to Danni, who scrambled up the wall like a girl in a circus. And it was a good feeling. Tom could take her weight, Tom could pull her in, Tom was the safe pair of hands.

He jumped when the urinal suddenly flushed on automatic, end of good moment, but as he helped her in, he saw the smoothness of her arms, clear apart from the old bruises, no needle marks.

He looked a second too long. 'No *narktyk,*' Danni said, 'see?'

'What you on about?'

'This was warning. Next time, hard stuff. This gang they say first time is weak.' She smiled at him, but grimly. 'Not hooked,' she said.

'Terrific.' Meanwhile, the lavatory wasn't the nicest place to talk about anything; he had to find them a better base. The church hall had an office that was used by its four main users where they each had their own cupboard: the playgroup, the scouts, the guides and the drama group. But as Tom led Danni in there he realised that this was the first room a user would head for coming into the building. If the drama group director came looking for scripts, she'd come straight in here to her cupboard, five seconds from the main door – and there was no other way out of the room.

But, thinking drama group, Tom had a brilliant answer. 'Come on.' He couldn't keep the smile off his face as he led Danni down the hall and up onto the small stage – where the set was still standing for the

Somerthorpe Players' production he'd seen with his mother, *Flare Path* – a pretend hotel lounge with a table, chairs and a comfortable sofa.

'See? Fully furnished!' he said. Going into the wings, he found the curtain pulleys that closed off the set from the hall and he pulled them shut. He opened his arms for acclaim; sort of, what more could anyone want?

But Danni wasn't so pleased. 'Not staying!' she said. 'Soon we go.'

'Soon we go,' he repeated. He punched a couple of cushions into being soft and made the sofa comfortable.

She was prowling the stage, restless, clicking her fingers like castanets, making that sound in her throat. 'Soon, please, the dark!'

'Yeah.' But they still had the best part of a day to get through. 'So, tell us about that paper... In the bag.'

Danni sighed, and shrugged.

'But only if you want.'

'Do not want. But do not mind.' She shrugged again. 'My father, he dies when I am baby. Him I do not know, just photograph, some things. But he has uncle. Not uncle, *old* uncle...'

'Great-uncle?' Tom tried.

'Like grandfather but grandfather brother; uncle.'

Tom nodded. 'Yeah, great-uncle.' He had one himself, his nan's brother, Uncle George, a smoker who always had to be asked to use the garden.

'My father – his father, grandmothers, grandfathers, all killed in war...'

The same as one of Tom's great-grandfathers, drowned on the *Hebe*, a minesweeper in the North Sea.

'...Auschwitz. Concentration camp. And Matka, my mother, she is orphan girl, cygan – you say gypsy – they are her family. But this man...you say great-uncle...sends to my mother in Warsaw this paper. Family name is on it, and this also is with it...' Danni lifted the silver eagle on its neck chain, showed it to Tom again on her fingers, then took it off and let him hold it.

'Yeah, cool. Is it valuable? Precious?' He rubbed his fingers together, saying 'money'.

Danni took it back pulling a face: she didn't care. 'Is in my hand for sleeping.' She showed how she clutched it to her chest in the night, before stringing it back round her neck. 'And the paper...' now she fished in her pocket and brought out the squared paper; '...the top, the name is here, from where it is coming.' They looked at it together. On closer inspection Tom could see that the paper was torn off a sheet; and in blue ballpoint and old-fashioned loopy writing he saw what Swain had read out the night before, '*RF 303 White House*' and that string of letters looking about as foreign as most of what he read: '*Bronislau Mikawski.*'

'That's got to be a postcode,' Tom said, 'that first bit. England or America, because it's written in English. That's where the White House must be, at this RF 303 place.'

'We run from drug gang, out of Warsaw to country people but everyone scared of gangs. We go to Gdansk, where there is this Harry.' Danni pursed her lips up to spit, but she didn't – and suddenly, as if she were bored with her story, she went on fast and matter-of-fact. 'Matka she has no family, my father has no family – gypsies we are not wanted in Poland; killed in war, slaves after. So Matka comes to England with this man, perhaps we find this White House, perhaps here is family.' Danni dumped herself down on the dummy staircase, looked all around, wanted out, and soon. 'This is what Matka thinks.'

'And your Matka, she shacked up with Harry who was a slave driver himself – both of you working for him and his sister?'

Danni didn't move, stared across the stage at him. 'Till she die.' Still very matter-of-fact.

'Does Harry know about your piece of paper?'

Danni hunched her thin shoulders. 'In darkness,

people they say things.'

In darkness? 'So...they...?' Tom wasn't quite sure how to ask this. But he guessed there was no way a man like Harry would risk a big fine and his job bringing Matka across from Poland just out of the kindness of his heart. He'd have wanted some sort of payback reward, like sex.

Danni read his mind. 'Marry. He marry her.'

Marry! Tom stared at her. 'That means you're his daughter? Half. Step.'

A question that had Danni up stiff and rigid, her face draining itself of colour. 'Never, *never* I am his daughter! *Never, never, never!*' Her face was twisted, on the edge of violent. 'He is monster!'

'Sorry, Dan.' Tom broke away to sit at a small table – sitting down took the edge off a situation, there was no eyeball to eyeball. He looked round the stage set, the wartime hotel. Danni was left standing angry in front of the short flight of steps, supposed to be leading upstairs. Now she said something fierce in Polish and suddenly sat down on them again, hunched – and thrust out her left hand pointing to the third finger. 'She wears ring here. *Left* hand.'

'Like my mum.'

'Does not count! In Poland is *right* hand for wedding ring...'

'Ah. I get you. So in her heart Matka never married

that man.' Tom nodded his understanding. 'But in the law she did…' And it suddenly hit him. 'So you're not illegal at all!'

Danni shrugged, still looking at her hands. 'Who care? I want back where I am free!'

And another sudden thought came to Tom; it caught him like a surprise punch and sat him up straight. 'Listen, if that's what Matka wanted… If we can't get you on a ship tonight why don't we have a go at finding your White House? Wherever RF 303 is? There might be contacts there for when you go back home. They might know other people. Or they might be family, like she reckoned…'

Slowly, Danni looked up. 'Yes, is what Matka want,' she said. 'But is hard.'

'Well, there's got to be a way of finding where a postcode is.' And suddenly, while trying to give the girl hope, Tom was filled himself with the thought that anything *was* possible – a rare thought for a kid like him.

She must have thought so, too, because she got up from her steps and came over to him. 'I try to go,' she said. 'But if not you will help me.' It wasn't a question, it was what would happen.

'Sure I will.' He smiled, the Tom Robinson Welton smile for female police officers and others. 'But I'm not clever, Dan. Not in my own language. You've got two, I haven't even got one properly.'

'Bollocks!' Danni said, and they both exploded a laugh into the other's face.

'See – you've learnt English quick over here!'

'I listen. I look. Also, I learn in Poland, sell to tourist.'

Tom looked at his watch. There were still hours to go, but things had suddenly turned a bit easier, all at once there was a new side to being here with the girl. But he wouldn't milk it. 'I'll go for some food,' he said, 'get you a proper meal, you've only had bits and pieces since the fish and chips. Build you up in case you go.'

'*When* I go!'

'Sure.'

'You be fast, uh?' she asked.

'Sure. I'll be back before you can say – cheese.' Just the way his mother used to talk to him as a little boy, except he'd nearly said 'knife'! Tom put his hand on her arm. 'I tell you what, you haven't got Matka, but you're not on your own while I'm around.'

She looked into his eyes. Had he touched her, inside? How did she feel about his commitment to her, whether she went or stayed?

'Food. Then we go, uh?'

'Sure. Then we go.' With a determined step Tom went off the stage and down to the exit at the back, the one the Somerthorpe Players used as a stage door. He rapped his V for victory on the woodwork. Dot, dot, dot, dash. And just for luck he did it again, dot, dot, dot, dash.

'The code won't be long,' he said.

'No. Do not.'

'Poland!' Philip Swain said. 'Polish!' He held the crumpled purple banknote between his fingers.

'Never been there,' Emma Thorpe replied. 'And never wanted to.' She was brushing Molly after her ride. 'Where'd you get it?'

'In the tack room. Where Thom-as was, and the bag he left behind, and the paper with the name and address on it. This was crumpled up under some straw. *What* was he doing here?'

'He heard the dogs barking, came to check for intruders.'

'Huh! A likely tale!'

Emma went on brushing vigorously. 'You don't actually think he's up to something with me?' She shot a look at Philip over the mare.

'No! Why should I?'

'Because he's not! As if!'

'Not you – and *him*! No, he's up to something with somebody else…'

Emma changed flanks, and came around to give

Molly a heavy grooming on her cousin's side. 'He told me he was taking a boy sailing…'

Philip Swain snorted. 'He definitely had someone or something down in his beach hut, and he had someone or something in the tack room. His face looked like sunstroke when I gave him the bag. I tell you, he's up to something with someone…'

'From *Poland?*' Emma's voice had a leather-knife edge to it. She smacked Molly's rump as she finished grooming.

'Don't know. But I'll find out. Next time I see him, I'll follow him and find out what he's up to.'

'Don't be beastly. What on earth for?'

'Oh, give me something to do; I've more or less finished my project.' He stood in the doorway and looked at Emma. 'Besides, you'd rather like to know, wouldn't you?'

'I couldn't care less. Asking him to Fressingfield wasn't my idea. But if you've got nothing better to do…'

Philip Swain smirked at his cousin. 'No, I don't think I have,' he said. 'I like decoding people's behaviour and exposing it…'

CHAPTER ELEVEN

Streetmap dot com. That was the website Tom had seen Emma Thorpe use for finding out where Molly was going to jump. She'd enter the postcode and the website would print up a local map with an arrow pointing to the place. Handy, or what? If he could get on to that website and ask it for RF 303 he'd be as good as walking up to the front door of the White House. Yes! Feeling good again, Tom ran from the church hall down to the local Spar shop for a cold chicken breast and a couple of brown rolls; plus a Mars bar that Danni had liked on Saturday, a carton of milk – and a toothbrush. Thoughtful, that, he reckoned. He gave Pauline at the checkout a five-pound note held like a paper V in his fingers the way his father did. He was going to get through his savings like water through a fishing net, but so what – he could splash it for that girl; and thinking of *streetmap dot com* was definitely a winner, she'd be impressed. Dot, dot, dot, dash! On a high he almost told Pauline to keep the change.

But he wasn't ten steps out of the shop door before he was ruffling his hair again, the most ruffled hair in Suffolk. Problem! Big problem – it should have hit him in the face as soon as he'd thought *internet*. They weren't on it. His dad wouldn't have it at home and they didn't let you onto it in the public library: also, he wasn't buzzed by mobiles and texting – him, texting! So how was he going to log on to Emma's handy website?

Ruffle, ruffle. And a sick surge in Tom's stomach told him there was one dead obvious way. He spat into the hedgerow at the nasty taste that had suddenly come into his mouth. He could do it through Emma herself. Which was a really gross thought because he'd have to pretend he was still the old Tom come scraping for a kind smile. But her place *was* on the way back...

Should he do it?

Could he?

Mrs Thorpe answered the door. 'Tom,' she said, looking at the Spar bag, 'are we out of things?' It was the way his mother sometimes worked, sending Tom to the house with the cleaning materials she needed.

'No, Mrs Thorpe, it's ordinary shopping, for home. I just wanted a word with Emma, please. Passing.'

'Ah.' Mrs Thorpe was clearly thinking through

Emma's head as well as her own. *Would Emma want a word with him?*

'Wait there.' Mrs Thorpe went away and didn't come back. But after a while Emma came, frowning, her head on one side, a slow arrival along the length of the dim hall.

'Yes?'

'Hi, Emm.'

'Hi. Yes?' She, too, looked at the Spar bag.

'Shopping. From Spar.'

'Not from Poland?'

Which winded him like a whack to the belly. *Poland!?* 'No, Spar.' Tom would never know how he got the words out. Philip Swain must have told her about the bag and the paper but she'd punched 'Poland' at him as if she'd saved it up. A grudge punch. 'My dad,' Tom found himself saying, 'he's got some old sailor friend from Poland – matter of fact, that's partly why I've come.' *Quick thinking! Going about! Duck your head as the boom comes across...*

'Go on.'

'Well, we're not sure where he lives. But I've got a postcode. And I wondered if you could get it up on your internet...' *Run with the tide now, nothing to lose...* 'Do us a favour?'

Emma stared through him. 'Do I owe a favour?' The lady of the manor talking to a lesser rank, the boy whose mother worked for hers. He had really upset her by not jumping at the chance of going with her to the Fressingfield show.

'No, it's the other way round as it goes,' he said.

Her eyebrows asked why?

'I'm sorry I couldn't come to Fressingfield and I owe you for that; which is the other reason I've come – to say sorry again.'

Emma half turned away. 'You said it once. Anyhow, Fressingfield was a mother's idea, not mine.'

'I know, you said she wanted me to help.'

'No, not *my* mother's idea, *yours…*'

'What?' Tom was still on the flagstone in the front porch, he'd got nowhere over the threshold; now he took a step back. '*My* mother's idea?'

'Sure. Your mother asked my mother if my mother would ask you to come out with us sometime – to cheer you up, take you out of yourself, she was worried about you being so upset over your holiday work…'

'I'm not upset, it's going magic.'

'Well that's fine, then. Now, what was it you wanted?' Emma snapped her fingers the way she brought her dogs running.

'Erm, this postcode…' God, what a smacker! What a dozo he was to get the wrong message from Emma. Of course she wouldn't want to go out with him.

'Oh, yes. Well, I can't do it now, Philip's on the computer printing up his dissertation. But I suppose we could fix five minutes sometime...'

'Thanks.' Tom ruffled his hair. 'And it's me asking, Emm, not my mum.'

'I appreciate that,' Emma said. And she cracked a quick smile at him. 'How about four o'clock?'

'Yeah, that'd be fine,' Tom said. 'Thanks.'

'No prob. Very well, then.'

Emma Thorpe shut the door swiftly, leaving Tom to turn away and face yet another direction. Forget Tom the man, the grown-up guy with a girl hanging on each arm: he was still his mother's backward little boy for whom things had to be done and arrangements made behind his back. *No prob!* Emma said. Well, no prob to her perhaps, but a big prob kick in the privates for him.

He walked back towards the church hall, out into Glebe Lane with the chicken breast, the Mars and the milk all drooping cold in the Spar bag that had no swing to it any more.

And behind him, quietly on the grass verge, Philip Swain followed, keeping his head below the level of the hedge.

Like a Somerthorpe Player going in through the stage door, Tom tried to whip himself into role again – that same freedom fighter back from another mission, but this time there was no way he could feel the hero. This time he was the traitor who 'used' people, the agent playing a double game. He tapped his code on the door but it should have been 'A' for 'ashamed' instead of 'V' for victorious. He'd lied about some friend of his father, he'd kept Danni his secret, he'd stopped being the upfront Tom Robinson Welton people could trust: and how short would he sell the Polish girl if Emma Thorpe really flashed her eyes at him? Because he was sick to the stomach that it wasn't her who'd asked him to Fressingfield. Dot-dash!

He gave Danni the bag of food. She hadn't sat there watching the clock go round, she'd found the hall kitchen down at the side of the stage. On the counter she'd set two plates with knives and forks, and salt, pepper and a couple of mugs. He looked at her, but her you-dare! stare back at him made him keep his mouth shut – about the domestic arrangements.

'I only got the one,' Tom said as the chicken piece came out. And he was sorry that he hadn't bought two – it would have been special, a meal together, partners over plates; but his thinking had been solo – Danni, Tom, Emma, Swain, one and one and one and one: and, anyway, he was too 'down' to relax over food. Dash-dot, dot.

Danni shrugged, he could please himself; and

without a word she cleared the counter. 'Later, I eat,' she said.

'I've got a bit of a result,' Tom told her. 'I'm getting onto the internet at four o'clock to find the postcode.'

'You have it, at home?'

'No, I have it – at a friend's.' And again Tom suddenly balked: but why couldn't he say who was helping him? Danni knew about Emma, she'd hidden in her tack room, she'd 'borrowed' her bike. Emma wasn't his girlfriend or anything, she was a girl from school, his mother worked for her mother; why shouldn't Danni know he'd just been to see her? But still he couldn't allow himself to say her name. 'Bloke called Philip Swain, he's good at all that sort of thing.'

The girl accepted it without question. 'Then soon we go!'

'Yup, as soon as we can, you bet! Six o'clock, on the bus, after I've seen Swain.' He'd worked it out; by the time they got into Lowestoft the place would be packed with people come in off the beaches and the trips. But, oh God, she was still the Danni who'd kissed him, twice, who'd let him comfort her, she hadn't changed since then. So why couldn't he admit to her that he was working with another girl on the postcode – for her sake? Would he go Mirror red if he said Emma Thorpe's name? Was he frightened Danni would be jealous?

'There was a Polish bloke in the play.' He snatched at anything to help pass over this stupid moment.

'*Nie rozumiem*. Not understand.'

'The play here.' A change of scene: Tom led Danni along from the kitchen up the steps and through the gap in the curtain to the stage. 'Where you're staying,' he tried to joke. 'See, this is supposed to be a hotel near an airfield and there's airmen and their wives staying here – and one of them's Polish. Mum brought me to see it to help with my project. A bit of Watson's beet farm at the back of us used to be an airfield. Anyhow, it had a Polish airman in it, the play, he spoke funny English, made people laugh...'

'Stupid people!'

'Yeah, you're right.' But Tom wasn't letting it go; he still felt as lumpy as school custard, no way could he talk about him and her. 'See, the pictures on the wall...' He waved a hand at the Wellington bombers and the aircrew smiling in front of them; and did he want four o'clock to come fast!

On the dot of four Tom was on Emma's doorstep. She was waiting for him – and was it his mixed-up state or did she look special again? She was in a fresh white sleeveless blouse with a blue ribbon in her hair; what wouldn't Danni give to have a change of t-shirt? And instead of her stable breeches she was in denim shorts; wouldn't Danni love to lose those tight joggers and get the air to her legs?

'Come in,' Emma said. 'Philip's gone out somewhere, we'll get your business done.' Tom followed her into the house, no sign of Mrs Thorpe, up the wide staircase and into what the family still called the nursery. 'Have you seen him?'

'Who?'

'Philip.' Emma looked sideways at him; but Tom only saw the table where Swain's typed and bound project was lying.

'Nope.'

The computer was already on, a screensaver scrolling shots of Emma jumping Molly.

'Sit down.' Emma pulled the office chair back for Tom.

'No, you.'

'No, you, it's your father's friend. Get online. Click on the internet icon.' Still Emma seemed to be looking more at him than at the computer.

But symbols he was happy with. Tom did as he was told. The dialling dib-dib-dibs did their stuff and the internet home page came up. Emma slowly spelt out the website address which Tom hunted down one-fingered and she bent over him to press 'enter' – all quite natural – and suddenly Tom was holding his breath so as not to smell the strawberry of her hair;

trying not to be the all-round traitor.

'What is it?'

I'm a shit. 'Nothing, I'm fine.'

'I mean, what's the postcode?'

'RF 303.' Now Tom's fingers were shaking slightly over the keyboard, the classic can't-do-anything feeling that hit him when he panicked, the situation he was in a million times a day.

'Enter it, then, if you please.'

If you please. It was the sort of way Mrs Thorpe spoke to his mother; superior, the boss.

His head was up at the monitor and down at the keyboard like a coastguard caught between a chart and a radar screen.

'Come on, you can do it.' Now she was like a teacher, encouraging 'It's you thinking about it that does for you…' She leant over and pressed 'search'. And it was she who read out the result. *The query returned no matches, please try again.'*

'What's that mean?'

'It means they can't find this postcode; and it didn't look like one, I've got to say. You've got it wrong, or it's got a letter missing – or it's not British, it's the wrong pattern, the wrong shape – do you see?'

'Bugger!'

'Who said it was a postcode – your father or this friend of his?'

'My dad – yes. Yes, my dad did.' As he said it Tom saw the paper in his head. 'And it also said "The White House"…' He didn't want a nil result.

Emma frowned. 'This letter being the piece of paper Philip found in the bag?'

'That's right, a torn off part of it.'

'Phil's got a very suspicious mind.' Emma had drawn back and was looking at Tom again, like an art dealer holding a painting.

'Don't tell me – I know.'

She suddenly laughed, but not the funny sort. 'He thinks you're up to something!' Sort of, *how stupid!*

'Me? Wish I was. Cheer up the holidays, wouldn't it, having a secret?'

'And you haven't, of course?'

'I couldn't pull the wool over a baby's eyes.'

'So we try the White House,' Emma decided.

'Please.' And while Tom's heart thumped almost to the point of cardiac arrest his fingers keyed it in as she dictated the spelling.

CHAPTER TWELVE

Philip Swain was crouched at a tombstone. The back door to the church hall was ajar, the long bolt of the emergency exit loose near its securing hole. Quietly he crept to the door and pulled it open, lifting the bar to be sure the bolt didn't scrape on the concrete threshold.

The squeak of the door hinges could be heard in the kitchen, but there was no special knocking of a code. Danni put her head to the crack – and drew back fast when another boy came creeping into the hall and started staring all around, just for a moment looking like he might head towards the kitchen. But he stopped short and turned to look at the stage; and like a prowler in the night he went to the steps and climbed them to go in through the curtains. Now he was out of sight, this stranger, this danger – and there were two ways out of the building: the way the boy had come in and out through the lavatory window.

Suddenly Danni ran fast across the hall; but as she

ran her trainers yelped on the clean, polished floor. She made it to the lavatory and hid behind its door; in her hand the breadknife she had brought from the kitchen. Her face said what she would do if anyone came for her now.

The curtains were slowly pulled open to show the hotel scene – and a second or so later the boy came onto the stage from the side. His eyes searched out for the cause of the yelp, looked down the hall at her but couldn't see her through the crack of the door. He went frowning to the sofa to pick up a cushion with a head dent in it. Danni's head dent. He put it to his cheek as if checking whether it was warm. He lifted the car rug from the sofa, felt it in his fingers and sniffed it like a pervert. He looked around the hall again and went up to the table on the stage – where he picked something up; and putting the something into his pocket he crept towards the steps that were supposed to be going upstairs in the hotel.

So he gave the girl her chance. The second he was out of sight Danni turned back into the lavatory, climbed onto the sink and lifted the bar that held the window. Fast and silent like a snake through an air vent she pulled herself through the small opening, and landing awkwardly, hands first, she found her feet and scuttled into the bushes.

By which time Philip Swain had come down from

the stage and gone into the kitchen – where he found yet another bag of fresh food. With a shake of his head he came out of the kitchen to stand in the empty hall – before crossing to the men's lavatory where a window was banging and where a knife was twisting a slow roulette on the tiled floor. From his pocket he took what he had found on the table of the hotel, held it up in front of him and dangled it.

'Oh, Thom-as!' he said.

Emma's printer was chugging out a map. Tom sat on one chair, Emma on another as the map emerged, the first of the White House locations from the long list the website had given, the nearest one that they'd chosen for starters – a place somewhere between the A14 and the A1156 in the north west suburbs of Ipswich. As it finished printing Emma looked at it, folded it and gave it to Tom.

'Well I hope that helps your father find his friend.'
'Thanks.'

'But the postcode's going to be IP for Ipswich, so if this is the place God knows where he got RF 303 from. Perhaps it's a car…? Or a phone code?' Her voice was bored, she really didn't care.

'Yeah, could be.' Tom didn't know what to think. This wasn't what anyone could call a result, just the nearest off the list of White Houses that Emma had taken from the screen. 'Well, it's over to the old man now.'

Emma said nothing but led him downstairs to the front door. Outside in the hazy sun Tom squinted; staring at a screen made the eyes go big.

While in the bushes dividing the church grounds from the manor house just across Glebe Lane another pair of eyes was squinting – Danni's; she was crouching among the fallen cones beneath a fir tree. As she watched, Tom and the girl from the house came out onto the front path. Danni's squint became a frown.

'Just a tip, Tom. Have more belief in yourself. You can do a bit more than you think.' The lady of the manor with a peasant.

Tom looked at the ground: no result with RF 303 and this White House map in his hand just one of a list as long as his arm; probably useless. Anyway, Danni would want to be away on the first safe ship.

'Cheer up! Your father won't cry himself to sleep, will he?'

'No.' Tom looked her in the cool eye, ruffled his hair and tried to smile his crooked smile. Whatever the snarled up reason was, he felt rotten lying to anyone, it wasn't his style – and he'd just deliberately denied having a secret. He made a move to go.

'Oh. So don't I get a thank you?' Sort of, *where's your manners?*

He was just about to say it; but she stood there looking so superior and untouchable that Tom had to do it. What the rough peasant doesn't do to the lady of the manor. What the butler doesn't do to the queen. He leant forward and kissed her on the lips. 'Ta, Emm,' he said. Real cheek.

And Emma just blinked.

At the sight of which, Danni, with eyes narrowed beneath the fir tree, growled, '*Srać! Zdrajca!*', spat into the ground and suddenly ran bent double through the tombstones and towards the road.

With the folded White House map in his hand Tom pretended to walk along Glebe Lane towards his house, but when he could he took the first break in the wire fence through into the churchyard and headed for the church hall.

He would have liked a fortnight to get there, tons of time to think himself straight before he tapped V for victory to get back in to Danni. He kept trying to tell himself that he owed her nothing; more the other way, everything he was doing was to help her; she was a kid on the run from a rotten stepfather and Tom was being her ally. Then why did he feel so Judas, just because Emma had tangled his rigging again? Because she had. He'd half liked that kiss, hadn't he? And she hadn't slapped his face. But the face in his head was Danni's; so he wanted the strawberry of Emma's hair out of his memory before he returned to the Polish girl.

Too soon he came to the back door of the church hall; and stopped short. It was open – wide open – and he hadn't left it like that, he'd left it looking closed. Like a cat at a bird's nest he came to the threshold. Now he could see right into the back of the stage with the theatre curtain flapping open in the daylight, definitely not looking right. *What the hell was going on here?*

He crept first to the kitchen – and Danni wasn't there. But across the hall the doors to both lavatories were open: was she in the Women's? She had to go sometimes, everyone does.

But something turned Tom to face the stage. The hotel set had someone on it, walking down from the upstairs landing: and it wasn't Danni. It was Philip Swain, smiling like a king who's had a traitor brought before him.

'Thom-as!'

'Swain.'

'So, what's all this? What's your little secret, eh? I've known you're up to something since Saturday...'

Words failed. Tom stood dumb.

'Secret food, secret papers, secret Polish money. Secret postcodes. And someone secret who was in here when I came, who got out secretly through a secret exit…' Swain's head cocked for an answer as he came down the steps at the front of the stage towards Tom. 'Eh, Thom-as?'

'I can't tell you. It's secret!'

'Don't be funny. Nothing to do with a mystery alien off the Seal Point rocks by any chance?'

'Not by any chance.' Tom stood his ground. Swain was in the open – he'd been talking to Emma, reading the papers, listening to the radio – but now Tom could get to grips with this because the boy really knew nothing. He wouldn't have been asking questions; Swain never asked questions when he could tell you what he knew, the cocky sod. He was fishing. So, say nothing. Give nothing away. Let him wonder.

'Does Emma know about your secret?'

Tom nearly said no, which would be falling into a trap – because that would have been saying he *had* a secret. But he held himself in, mouth shut tight. Until Swain took something out of his pocket, something Tom recognised.

'The Players won't be pleased to know you've been skulking around mucking about with their props.'

'What props?'

'From the play.' Now Philip Swain held it up, let it swing, tantalised. It was Danni's silver eagle on its chain.

'That's not…'

'Oh yes it is, it's from the play. The jewellery eagle, the Polish airman's "wings". Must be worth a bit, hired, got to be returned…'

'Give it to me!' Tom made a grab for it.

'Certainly not. This is evidence, Thom-as. I'll give it back to the producer – and we'll see what she thinks about the cleaner's boy filching through her things…'

Out of nowhere Tom aimed the punch that would flatten Swain, the nose-breaker he'd been asking for since forever. But Swain was quicker. He must have read Tom's eyes because he ducked the swing like an expert, and was legging it out of the hall before Tom had got his balance back from the missed swing.

By which time there was no more for Tom to do than swear and swear and swear, and put things straight and shut windows and doors before his mother next came to clean. Shite was never so scarce that Tom Robinson Welton wouldn't tread in it.

He ran home as fast as he could but Danni hadn't gone for the shed this time. His top hope was that he'd see her on the way, hiding in bushes or the hedgerow or over in the beet field; that she'd come running out of somewhere, or that she'd have left the red scarf hanging where he could see it so he could look around for her – any of those would do. But there was no sign of her, she'd been driven right off –

and what Tom really wanted to do was go back to Emma's, get Danni's eagle back and knock Philip Swain through a couple of walls.

The shed was empty of anything Danni, and it was a sad sight. The look of it, just the way it had been before, was like the end of a school holiday when you walked back into the same, boring classroom you'd charged out of before the break. And back in the house – because he had to put in an appearance now and again – the news was what he'd feared.

'They got that number,' George Welton told him.

'What number?' Tom asked. Playing innocent, because he knew.

'What Gull and the police are looking for. What he was talking to you about, the number off the sail...'

'Oh, yeah?'

'Two figures in the boat hidden by the sail but they've got its number.'

Now for it. 'And whose was it?' Wouldn't his dad have said if he knew it was Tom's?

'Dunno. But they've got it and they're checking with the Mirror people.'

Mirror dinghies had all their numbers listed by age and they kept tabs on ownership when people re-sold them. Yes, he would have said, and he didn't know. But, anyway, this was all in the past. Tom had saved the girl off the rocks but now she'd gone, driven off by Philip Swain. He could get into trouble for sailing on his own and for lying to the police, but he could wriggle his way out of that with secret girlfriend talk – say he'd taken someone like Emma Thorpe for a sail. And that would be the end of it – because he wasn't harbouring Danni any more. He was off the hook where she was concerned.

So why the blue devils inside?

And he knew very well it was because he didn't *want* to be off Danni's hook.

Luckily, after they'd had their tea the Weltons all went their own ways; George Welton to the Yacht Club, Joyce Welton to the little room upstairs where she sometimes did a bit of tapestry, Sally to the big armchair and *The Simpsons* – and Tom Robinson Welton to Lowestoft on his bike. He reckoned he knew where Danni had gone: she wasn't in his shed so she'd be chancing it and going for a ship. But Tom didn't shout up to his mother *where* he was going, just that it was out for a ride, and on a light summer night his mother didn't ask where.

Tom's bike knew the way on its own; but this time he didn't bother with a baseball cap and windcheater, he pedalled sixty to the minute in a high gear and just kept his head down. But how would Danni have got to Lowestoft? Bus – it had to be bus, unless she'd hitched a lift. She knew where the bus ran, and if she'd got no money she'd spin the driver some tale, give him a name and address where they'd never find her. Tom wouldn't be fast enough to overtake a bus but he had to catch her up before she jumped a ship. He had to say goodbye; he had to tell her he'd get her eagle necklace back and send it to her one day. And he knew where to hang about to see her; somewhere between the railway bridge, the warehouse, and the quayside – he knew when she'd come, as soon it started to get dark. But he had to make sure he didn't get seen by Harry first.

Tom wasn't much good with scripted words, he'd never be able to read and learn a part – but he was a fair old actor when he needed to be. After he'd locked up his bike and started slinking along the commercial road from the station to the quayside he saw a stick just the other side of a netted wire fence; more a slender pole about two metres long. It was in a yard filled with all sorts of flotation stuff, rusting marker buoys, old life belts and cork and canvas jackets. If he could reach that stick and pull it through he could make it look like a fishing rod until anyone got up close. Why skulk and hide – why not sit dangling his feet over the quayside and pretend he was fishing for eels? With his head down staring at the water he'd be like a film extra, a natural part of the scene.

He took the stick and walked on with it over his

shoulder, still straining his eyes in all directions. There were fewer people about in the evening – no one, in fact, apart from a shadowy figure busy on the bridge of the ship. And it was just the one ship that was there tonight, not a vehicle or container ship but a freighter with nothing on her deck – no yellow lorry, she'd probably brought in timber in her hold. It could be going out or have recently come in, but it would be a definite target for Danni.

Playing his part, he sat on the edge of the quay and held out his stick like a fishing kid. Fishing had never been his thing, he preferred action on the water to sweet fanny happening beneath it, fishing people had too much time to sit and think. But it was thinking he did right now, asking himself what Danni would be doing; and colouring in his own pictures.

She'd have come to Lowestoft on the bus and got herself tucked away somewhere in the town – there was a multi-storey car park with loads of dark corners; there were public lavatories; there was a supermarket where she could wander the aisles and eke out time; there was a cinema she could get into, a couple of hours in the dark for a quick kid dodging in. And there was the railway station with a waiting room, a siding with a carriage in it, a line of railway trucks for playing the hobo; there were all sorts of places where she was this minute. But as soon as dusk fell he knew she'd come sneaking across the bridge or along the road, and with a hide-and-seek crouch and a run at the gangplank, she'd be onto the ship and getting herself under a tarpaulin in a lifeboat. Sure, Tom had it all pictured in his head.

He looked up at the ship, all flaky metal and rusty rivets up close, and he read its name. And was that an omen or not? The name of the ship was the *Sea Eagle*. Eagle lost, eagle found! So if he could sit here and wait, although Danni would be past being helped by him he could at least say sorry to her for rotten Philip Swain and wish her luck for the rest of her life.

The water sucked between the *Sea Eagle* and the quay. A jetty light across the dock came on and jigged on the water. A fish splashed nearby and for a second Tom thought he'd got a bite – if he'd had a line! Beneath the smooth surface he saw layers of slowly swirling silt and across the top of it the chill of a late summer evening shivered him. *What was he up to?* He was miles from home on a stone quayside catching cold through his bum waiting to whisper something to a girl he'd known five minutes. And what, boy, would that whisper be in the precious seconds he'd have? *Cheers! Good luck! Write to me, I'll get you your eagle back...* Why was he here just to do that?

Why? No question. There wasn't any doubt any

more, there hadn't been any doubt since he knew she'd gone from the church hall; the way he'd felt had told him the truth. Emma might be pretty, Emma might be nice, Emma might be sexy; no boy he knew would be upset by a smile or a touch or a friendly kiss from Emma Thorpe. But coming here tonight with Harry around somewhere, risking what he was risking for Danni, Tom knew very well the reason why he was doing it. It was because if he wanted anyone in the world to smile at him or touch him or give him a friendly kiss it was Danni. Or just to say she liked him, that's all he wanted to hear before she went. OK, Emma Thorpe was instant attraction, but Danni with her trust and her spirit, she grew on you, she went deeper. It was so clear now; she wasn't fantasy, she was for real.

Now Tom's heart felt full, his head felt light; and all he wanted was to have time for a proper goodbye. So wouldn't it be stupid catching her here on the quay as she made the last part of her run at stowing away? He needed to be further back, in the lee of the warehouse or underneath the iron steps of the railway footbridge, he needed a few seconds of precious time with her somewhere in the shadows.

He looked around. The dusk was gathering fast so he could hide up better now; do what Danni would be doing, moving about.

Still clutching his stick, Tom eased himself up, walked slowly at first then suddenly scuttled for the underside of the bridge steps. And watching, listening, crouching in scrub like a spear-carrying hunter he waited. His legs tingled, then they ached; he wanted to pee – and he pee'd; his eyes hurt with the looking and his ears hummed with the strain of listening. His watch marked the ticking of five minutes, ten, fifteen, twenty-five; he started thinking of how long he should give it before going home. And then for no apparent reason he sensed something happening, there was a change in the atmosphere, a static charge; his skin prickled up, a nerve twitched in his arm; that same wavelength from outside his shed the night before told him that Danni was near.

And from his hiding place near the railway he saw her. He'd been right, he'd read her mind. She was creeping across the lines of the railway track, bent double as she stepped over them. The trains here were diesel, there were no electric rails or overhead cables, and the wide expanse of eight or ten tracks was empty. She was crossing the same way they'd come together but she was on the ground this time, parallel with the footbridge, and when she got to the fence on this side she'd be only metres from where Tom was waiting. Already he was planning how to help her over and going over the words of what he'd say, because he *would* say something. He felt deeper, painfully deeper about this girl creeping across in the red headscarf than he felt about anyone else in the world. It could sound as stupid as anything he'd ever said but he was going to tell her, 'Danni, I love you' – tell her that first and then say the other stuff. But 'I love you' would be the most important words ever.

She came on, he saw her eyes glinting once in the railway lights as she made her careful way towards the fence. And Tom moved, just showed himself – and she stopped. She looked straight at him and he opened his mouth to mouth 'I love you' at her.

But her mouth was already open. 'You are shit!' she spat at him. 'Srać!'

CHAPTER THIRTEEN

Him? Not Tom, he wasn't shit, he wasn't *srać*, he didn't deserve to be spat at. She had to think he was Harry lurking in the shadows.

'No, it's Tom!' he whispered back. 'Tom Robinson Welton – and I love—'

'Tom is srać!' She pushed him off and grabbed the concrete upright of a supporting post, stuck a toe into a diamond of the fence and pulled herself over.

'Danni!'

'English shit!'

'Why, shit?' He hadn't stolen her eagle; he hadn't made her run away from the church hall, that had been Philip Swain. All he'd ever done had been for the best, for her. He grabbed at her arm but she wrenched it away, spat out, 'Go kiss that girl!' and zigzagged across into the warehouse shadows near the gangplank of the ship.

So that was it! She'd seen him at the door with Emma, she knew he'd lied about it being Swain who was helping on the internet – and she'd seen him kiss Emma as he came away. All true. But not the truth of how he felt inside. No way! And she had to know that, he had to put himself straight. She was seconds from going out of his life forever, but how could he let her go with that shit opinion of him? How could he let it end like this? He'd never be able to be in the beach hut or his shed or the church hall or talk to Charlie Gull without thinking of her.

But if she thought about him what would she be thinking? Two-timer! Traitor! Which he wasn't – and he had to tell her, he had to!

Which was one thing he couldn't do. Standing there he was hit by the sudden awful, gutting fact: that there was no way he could put it right, because if he came out of hiding to run, or if he shouted after her as she went for the gangplank, he'd have to show out – show both of them out – which could wake up the ship and get her caught; doing what he wanted could stop her doing what she wanted.

A terrible reality that hit him like a crack on the head from a swinging boom. If he wanted to put Danni first he had to let her go; he had to let her get to the ship still thinking the way she did. He had to stay silent, be misunderstood, let the truth go, put himself last. If he really cared about her, that was the sacrifice he had to make – the most painful lesson he'd ever had; here, tonight in the Lowestoft dusk; that that was what love was about.

He watched her creep towards the gangplank from the shadows. He watched as she crept across the narrow quayside between the warehouse and the ship. She didn't look back, and a pang of loss twisted his stomach as she suddenly ran up the narrow gangplank onto the deck; his last ever sight of her. As he watched Danni going...

To see her suddenly confronted by someone bursting out of the bulkhead door at the head of the gangplank. Grabbing her – a hand round her mouth, a fierce arm round her body: a man with silver oiled hair in the port light. Harry, her stepfather, who'd been hiding, waiting for her!

Danni kicked but she couldn't scream for the hand clamped on her mouth, she wriggled and squirmed but she couldn't free herself as the strong man half dragged and half carried her back down the gangplank and onto the quayside.

'Stop all this nonsense, will you? You're coming home, I've forgiven you, you're all right. See sense, girl – you come home with me where you belong!'

Now a second figure appeared at the bulkhead, the skipper no doubt who'd let Harry hide on his ship. He pulled up the gangplank and clanged shut the gap in the ship's side – while Harry changed his grip on

Danni to frogmarch her to the foot of the railway bridge, his hand still clamped over her mouth. He was forcing her home across the lines.

And there was nothing else for Tom to do. He ran out of the shadows and stood across the lowest steps of the bridge. If the man took her home there'd be no getting her out of a locked house. Her mother had been married to Harry; Danni was legally his step-daughter; her only chance of leaving him was by running, no one else could help.

'Get out the road, boy!'

'No! You let her go!'

'Don't be a stupid jerk, get out the road!'

'Let go of her!'

All the time Danni was wriggling, struggling and kicking; but the man came bullying on, and suddenly changing his grip to a throttling arm around her throat, he went to his pocket. A fumble, and out came a drivers' window hammer with a short steel spike. Danni screamed but there was no one to hear who would help, and with that lethal weapon raised Tom would have to get out of the man's way.

...To let him take her to the slavery she'd run from, to what had been so bad for her that she'd tried to kill him in the night; to what had made her jump ship into the killing North Sea rather than face again.

And Tom stood his ground. Terrified, his eyes on

the hammer, he stayed where he was. 'You let her go!'

'You'll have this, boy!' Harry raised the hammer higher at Tom – the thing would crack Tom's head like a bolt in a bird's egg when it came down.

He flinched. Sense said he had to turn and run, get help, get the police, at least make someone look at Danni's problem. She was choking, her eyes were bulging but she was pulling down at his clamping hand. Enough to speak, to croak.

'Stop him! Beast man!'

'If I can!'

'Please! He beats me!'

'Shut up!' Harry shook her. 'Little minx!'

What? So this trucker was handy, had a belt or a stick! Hammer or no, the thought of it buzzed Tom's brain, it rolled his stomach. As he saw Danni's face changing colour with the force of that arm round her throat clamping tighter he wanted to get at this monster. His palms were sweating; his right hand was slipping on the stick.

The stick! The thick stick! Two could use a stick!

'Get out of it, boy!'

'Let her go!' As Tom gripped the stick and brought it up to thrust it hard at the man's face, near the eyes. Reaction, straight and true, and the man couldn't get out of the way, he had to take it in the face or put up a hand to stop it. Jerking back he let go of Danni and wrenched at the weapon.

'You bastard!' He'd still taken a sharp blow to the cheek, a hard, spiteful poke. And Danni was free and running. Tom thrust again, the hammer had fallen, the man had limped off balance – but he wouldn't lose hold of his end of the stick. Young against old. In a last lunge with both hands Tom put all his sail-raising, dinghy-hauling strength into one more thrust before suddenly letting go to run pounding across the footbridge; the man not following because it was Danni he was chasing. The other way.

And Tom couldn't know whether or not the monster trucker caught up with her. She could have run off further into the docks or gone along the industrial road towards the railway station, he didn't know which. But as Tom came to the road beyond the bridge he clung to the thought that she had to be quicker than that old man with his limp. Eyes skinned for both of them, Tom hurried through the town. It was still busy in the fish bars and cheap eats: ice cream lickers and stay-up kids strolling the Marine Parade. Darkness had fallen now and the flashing lights of evening entertainment strained Tom's eyes because he hardly dared to blink. He couldn't go back to the railway station for his bike, that was too central; so he skulked around the outer streets in the hope of seeing her; but in the end when getting home any later would mean a grounding he had to give up on Danni – and his bike – and make for the Somerthorpe bus shelter.

But all the way, every step, every breath – every thought was of what Danni had said. He probably beat her when she didn't do what he wanted, or if she wasn't quick enough, or she dropped a plate or said the wrong word, or looked at him the wrong way – then he punished her. He beat her; which was worse than even saying he hit her. No wonder she'd tried to knife him, the tyrant. *And he wouldn't want her back if he didn't like having his little Polish slave!* Or else he'd let her go, let her sink or swim or get on a ship, go away from England. No, his rotten aim was to get her back in the house, have her right where he wanted, where he could get up to all sorts, dominate her, scare her, work her, have her where he and his slimy sister could imprison her and go on beating her, now that her mother was dead.

Already, she could be back there, locked up in a room.

And that would be defeat, all round.

Like a licked foot soldier on the long retreat from the battlefield Tom came to the bus shelter. Where she was hunched with frightened eyes looking through the etched graffiti on a dirty window pane.

'Danni!'

She leapt up, she grabbed at him and pulled him to her in a fierce arm grip the way Harry had held on to her.

'Tom!'

And with his arms around her she buried her head into his chest, and cried, and cried, and cried.

With people going home from the pictures, the last bus was full; but Tom and Danni got two of the back seats near the emergency exit – because Harry hadn't gone away, so having two ways out of anywhere was handy. Tom held her hand; she was shivering and seemed smaller, a kid – and he couldn't get out of his mind what she'd said she'd had to take.

But Emma Thorpe was also in his mind and he had to get that straight; because he was very clear himself. Maybe he wouldn't say what he'd planned to say back in the shadows but he did have to put this important thing straight. 'That Emma Thorpe...I know her.'

'You kiss her. You say is boy but is girl, and you kiss her.'

'Well, she asked for it. I was shocking her, knocking her off her high and mighty perch...'

'But then you are brave tonight, you fight for me.'

'Yeah, I fight for you.'

'For what I tell you? This terrible thing?'

'No!' He turned, lifted her face to look at him. 'It wasn't what you said, or what he did. I fight for you anyway, Dan. Because you're...special.'

'Not!' she said.

'You're special to me. That other girl, I said it was a boy because I was worried you might be jealous about a girl...'

'Why jealous, me?' But there was a hint of tease in her voice.

'Perhaps I hoped you'd be jealous... I don't know about you.' He dropped his voice lower. 'But I know about me.'

'What, about you?' She was sitting up now, coming out of her scare, getting to be the sparky Danni again, just a bit.

And Tom couldn't not say it now, could he? So he did. He looked away out of the bus window, and he looked back at her again. 'About...the fact...that...I love you.' There was the catch of a breath, then a silence, before more and words came tumbling out all over one another. 'I didn't want you to be jealous of her so I pretended she was Philip Swain.'

Danni sat silent. The bus bumped along, quietened as people nodded off or just ran out of conversation. A word way down the aisle and everyone would hear it, so it wasn't the time for talk, but Tom badly wanted to know something. He'd laid himself bare –

so how did she feel about him?

There was no answer, in words. But she leant her head on his shoulder and quietly changed the way they were holding hands so her fingers entwined themselves between his, more intimate.

And for now he was very content with that.

CHAPTER FOURTEEN

They were back at the church hall, in through the lavatory window again. It was very late now but Tom had phoned home from the town bus stop to say his bike had got a puncture, he was walking from Pottonwick. He reckoned he'd be back by half-eleven – which gave him forty minutes with Danni to sort out his mixed up state of shock and sympathy over what she'd told him. Talking hadn't been easy on the bus; at the sound of the word 'love' the woman in front of them had half turned her head and they'd kept themselves quiet – holding hands and sitting close. Which was new to Tom, the long ride with Danni tight against him and her a girl who'd had stuff done to her; he almost felt the hairs growing on his body as if he were the sixth former who'd been expelled for going home with the art teacher.

Now he was sitting with Danni on the sofa used in the Air Force play – and he badly wanted to know what Harry had done, how long and often he'd been beating her. And why hadn't she told him before? But how did you get into that sort of talk – so he brought up the silver eagle.

'Philip Swain's got your necklace,' he said. 'He thought it was something they used in the play.' He looked round at the wartime 'hotel', the pictures on the scenery walls of airmen smiling bravely in the sun.

'Stupid. Is on cushion, then pot boils. Forget. But we get it back!' She said it with determination. 'Is in my family, was special for my father…'

'Sure. I'll sort out Swain!'

'My father, there is picture at my bed. He sells in markets but is not strong.' She shrugged her shoulders. 'Very cold in Warsaw. But good man. Not like the other, Harry. When he does beating I think how my father, he cry in heaven.'

Tom said nothing, he could only imagine Danni's hate and anger at what Harry did. He squeezed her hand. But she took hers away and sat formal, polite; perhaps such things had to be better coming out coldly.

'He make her marry him; she is scared for going back, for Danni to go back to drug gang. So she marry that man.' And a sudden turn to Tom with a fierce poking at her own chest. 'But not in the heart…'

Tom had to swallow.

'She marry. She sleep in same bed, she...'

Now Tom gave a quick nod to move her on. He didn't want her going into the details; he could never think of his own mum and dad having sex.

'Matka she is ill, a long time she is ill. She has cough, she has blood – but still he work her. Sometime I think he hit her, but she is scared, she say nothing. But when she die...he treat me like dog. Danni's head was lowered, her shoulders had dropped. 'He has belt, it hangs on door, and when he think I am bad he take belt to me, and he makes noise, like animal...'

'The bastard!' Tom took a chance and reached out a hand to turn her face to look at him. 'He wants you back before you tell anyone. Plus he likes the power, having a little skivvy slave he can knock about. But why didn't you tell me before?'

Danni was wet with tears, her eyes, her mouth; Tom found a tissue and wiped her face as dry as he could; but as he wiped more tears were coming. 'I am too proud,' she sobbed, trying to look like her words but failing. 'Ashamed to be whipped dog. And it gets worse if I go back. I am prisoner.' Danni suddenly gave a great groan like grieving and waved her hands to end the talk.

'You've got to hate men.' Simply said.

And she took an age to find the calm to turn to

him. 'Not all,' she said; 'Danni does not hate Tom.'

'Thanks.' He smiled, ruffled his hair. 'And I told you...about me... how I feel...'

She snuffled, shivered some more; and now they were holding one another tight, arms around shoulders and waists. And Tom wondered how he could keep the angry pounding inside him from bursting out of his body. To hold her tender while his insides raged made his breathing hard, loud, almost snorting.

'I'll tell you something,' he managed to say, 'you're never going back to Poland: not to some friend. You and me, we're going to find RF 303 and the White House, your dad's old family. *Family*! And if we don't, my mum and dad are going to adopt you.'

Danni found a bright white smile. 'So I am sister to you?'

'Oh, I definitely don't want that.' He hugged her harder, turned to kiss her, but she pulled away.

'Still this Harry is danger,' she said. 'No way for police to know I tell truth. He will say these marks are from Warszawa gang. So I say this, he say no. It is *my* saying, and *his* saying. He can point finger and say what he want about me: Danni is bad girl, thief, mad with knife, any damn thing he can say...'

'But they wouldn't make you stay with him...'

Danni was getting cross; of course she'd thought

through all this. 'He is father now. Legal. I say he is beast man. He says no. End of story.'

'So we've *got* to find your real family here.' Tom could be forceful, too. 'Which we are going to do, Danuta.' And the use of her full name made her smile, brought her back to him. 'But first...' Tom didn't want to look at his watch – but he wanted to look at his watch. 'It's late, I've got to get home. But you're safe here, till tomorrow. Then we'll crack on, early.'

Danni smiled. Her face was recovering from her anger and her crying, her breathing was losing its catches and gasps. She was able to calmly look him in the eye. 'And you will kiss me, please?'

There was no question about that. He kissed her, gentle and long and deep, coming away and murmuring, 'I love you, Danni,' into her soft breast. And they stayed in that warm embrace until he knew he had to go from the dark hall, out through the door behind the stage.

But as he went the girl whispered after him. 'Tom. True man,' she said. 'Jerzy Mikawski, like.'

'Jerzy Mikawski? Who's that?'

'My father.'

And Tom Robinson Welton went home with creation's fullest and warmest wind in his sail.

*

First thing next morning he was up ahead of his parents and out of the house early. For a start he had to get the necklace back from Philip Swain. He didn't want to go to Danni without it and he guessed Philip Swain would still have it – there hadn't been time to do much about it. He knew Swain and Emma would be about: people with horses and dogs lead a get-up-early sort of life.

It was Swain who saw Tom first. He was coming back from the fields with the dogs: who must have given him a bit of courage, seeing Tom coming towards him along Glebe Lane. The last time he'd met Tom he'd had a punch thrown at him.

'Thom-as!'

Tom eyed him. He had all the old neck in the world.

'What can I do for you?' Swain asked.

Had he forgotten yesterday? Did he think Tom had? Was he reckoning on the dogs saving him from a smack in the mouth? As it was, they hardly growled at Tom – he wasn't on their territory and they knew him.

'I want a word.'

'Any particular word? I can supply most.'

Don't let him get to you! Tom told himself. Swain's Swain, you won't change Swain – and if you want something off him you go about it in a Swain sort of way.

'Yeah, there is a particular word – "stealing"; or words, "stealing by finding".' It was one of Charlie Gull's favourite phrases for the parasites who swept family beaches with their metal detectors as the sun went down.

'And who's doing the stealing by finding might I ask?'

'You are. One silver eagle on a chain. You found it and you took it. That's stealing.' Tom had come within hitting distance, because if words failed he was going to deck this cocksure kid. He'd seen off Harry the trucker, he'd see this one off as well.

'Stealing from whom? The Somerthorpe Players? That's an RAF prop from the play.'

Tom stared him in the eye. 'Well it isn't, as it goes. It belongs to a private individual.'

'Ah. And who might that individual be, your mother – the cleaner?'

Which would suddenly be a neat answer for Tom. It'd be dead easy to say it was his mother's. But something held him off from that, just for the time it took him to work out how that lie might lead into deeper water. Or for the time it took Emma Thorpe to come trotting Molly out of the entrance to Watson's fields – which was what Tom saw beyond

Swain. Both of them watched her as she came up to them – blokes always did. She stopped Molly and stared down at Tom.

'Does the vicar know?' she asked him.

'That a dog collar's for life, not just for Christmas? Does he know what?'

Emma turned in her saddle to face the direction of the church hall; she pointed her whip that way. 'That you're hiding an illegal immigrant on church land?'

'Eh?'

'I think you heard me.'

Some sort of sunlight was warming Philip Swain's face, a denial was frozen on Tom's while his stomach turned.

'I've seen her,' said Emma with all her superiority – her sex, the saddle, her social class – and the surprise.

'Seen who?' Tom wasn't going to give in until the last plank gave out in his leaky boat.

'She didn't see me, I was hacking back along Watson's field, behind the yew hedge. She was hanging knickers on the top of a bush near the back door of the church hall. She keeps herself clean, I'll say that for her...'

'Say it for who?' Tom's final plank hadn't quite given yet; but it was about to go, any second.

'The girl you're hiding in the church hall,' Philip Swain put in. 'The girl who got out when I went in.'

And his face gleamed with the shine of a victory. 'And the girl who's lost a Polish eagle…'

Molly neighed and nodded as if she were in agreement; Emma steadied her as she pawed at the ground impatiently. 'The girl the radio's been on about, the girl from the sea, the girl picked up in a red-sailed dinghy, the illegal immigrant off the ship.' Emma said it all very matter-of-fact; and now she turned steel-cold. 'The girl you lied to me about, Tom Welton, the girl for whom you couldn't come to Fressingfield, the girl for whom you were finding a postcode saying it was about a friend of your father's. That girl, who hasn't got a change of clothes and has to hang her knickers on a bush.'

Tom blinked up at Emma, ruffled his hair; Swain wasn't in it, he didn't care about Swain, but it wasn't nice being found out by Emma; he had never liked lying to her. 'Why don't you help her out, then?' he asked.

'What?'

'Why don't you come down off your bloody high horse and I'll tell you about her, and you can see if you want to help her, too – or if you're like Charlie Gull and my dad and half Suffolk, pus-filled with prejudice.' Emma had surprised him, but he knew he was surprising her back, taking this line. For a moment it looked as if she might kick Molly and turn away. But she suddenly swung her leg over the horse's back and slid down to the ground.

'Be careful what you say, Tom Welton. If I know about it and Philip knows about it, we can't pretend we don't.'

'So it had better be good,' Philip Swain put in.

'Or bad,' said Tom. 'And it's very bad, if you want to listen.'

And he told them. Emma tethered Molly to a *Private Property* sign at the Watson's fields entrance and listened, first standing then sitting on the verge to hear Tom's story. Philip Swain lolled on a gatepost but eventually sat, too, as he listened to how Danni had been rescued from the outcrop and hidden up by Tom. Both of them sat grim-faced as Tom told them of Danni's exile, her mother's death and having to live with the trucker and his sister who treated her badly, forcing her to skivvy; and he got in about Harry's grab at Danni and the poke in the face with the long stick; he was still proud of that. He ended with, 'I'm helping her to find her family in England...' but the pair of them said nothing and simply stared: no move yet; no offer of help; a bit of sympathy on Emma's face but Tom knew he hadn't won them over, not enough for them to put themselves on the line.

'If they come here illegal don't they ask for what they get?' Emma said.

'You make your bed and you lie in it,' Swain had to add.

And Tom's anger flooded: the anger he'd felt at hearing what Harry had done to Danni; which he'd held back to leave her some privacy. But what boiled underneath was the thought of what else he might be trying to do if he got her back.

'He's been beating her. He's got a belt, and he uses it. He treats her like a whipped dog, worse than you'd ever treat an animal. She's his slave. Emm, she mustn't have to go back to him!'

The Suffolk air seemed so still. Seagulls called somewhere down at the harbour. High above the fields a small jet headed for Norwich airport. Molly jingled as she cropped at the grass.

Emma had shot a look at Philip Swain, who'd looked away from her; now she came back to Tom.

'Have you seen marks on her?'

'No! Nothing drastic.' And he was about to tell her about Harry blaming the Warsaw drugs gang for anything worse than the bruises when Philip spoke, eyes at the ground.

'They're careful about marking you, people like that...'

Again, the Suffolk quiet. 'We'll meet her, see where we go from there,' Emma said. 'Won't we?'

And, toughing something out, Philip Swain nodded

but still said nothing.

'I'll stable Molly and come back,' Emma said. 'You two go on.' She was always the boss.

Philip Swain was on his feet. 'You go in first, Tom, prepare the ground, then I'll come in and give her back her eagle.'

'You got it on you?'

The other boy nodded. 'Same trousers.'

For some reason Tom's throat felt swollen, his eyes sore, like after crying. Perhaps telling someone's secrets left you feeling like that. He nodded and as Molly was ridden away, he quietly led Philip Swain through into the churchyard and over to the hall. Neither of them spoke a word – but Tom's head was ringing to something already said. Philip Swain had called him Tom, not Thom-as: and all at once he felt like someone else.

CHAPTER FIFTEEN

Down at the harbour a wheeling seagull just missed Charlie Gull with a splat that would have given his black cap a summer touch of white. He headed for his little office which was tucked in under the rampart at the harbourside. He sat in there and flicked the switch on his electric kettle but long before it could boil there was a knock on the window of his door. A biggish, silvery haired man stood outside.

'Yes?' Charlie Gull leant to open up to whoever this was. He was always ready to shake his head when new holidaymakers asked if there were beach huts to be had.

But this man was tapping a rolled newspaper on his folding table. 'You seen this?' the man asked.

'Depends what it is. I have to ration my reading...' Charlie waved an arm at his busy world outside.

'The *Echo*. You Charles Gull?' The man started unrolling the paper.

Now Charlie smiled. 'Ah. That girl out of the

water. They never get it right in there but it's the gist.'

'It says here she was seen in a boat with a red sail and you're checking the number on it…'

'Factually correct,' said Charlie. 'At the time of going to press.' He looked at his watch. 'Except it's not me checking. But as we speak that's all been done.'

Now the man came right into the small office; he filled the doorway and Charlie had to sit back. 'Mind that kettle with your arm.'

'I've got a bit of personal interest, boy.' The man rubbed at a sticking plaster under his left eye.

'Oh, yes? What sort of personal interest? She's off a foreign ship, you don't sound – ' Charlie looked hard at the man. 'You're local, aren't you?'

'Lowestoft.'

'So, how can I help you? Only – ' Charlie checked his watch again, difficult in the cramped space.

'Foreign ship or not, I'm that girl's father.' The man seemed to grow bigger as he said it and Charlie tried to stand up but there wasn't room. 'You know kids, there was a row over sod all then it all got out of hand. She run off to the docks an' done something stupid. I just need to know where she is. I've got to get her back.'

Charlie rolled his mouth around as if he were finishing the sucking of a small boiled sweet. 'You want the police, then.'

'No, I don't want the police. Personal, my life is – I've never reported her missing, she ain't been named, has she? But you have, your name's in the paper an' it says you're onto the people who made the boat.' He rolled up the paper again.

'No, the woman policeman: she's the one dealing wi' the boat people.'

'Only, there was a kid involved, sailing the boat, wasn't there? "Tallish, dark brown hair"? That's in here.' He whacked the paper on the desk. 'Know anyone around here of that description?'

'Fits a few,' said Charlie. 'I can give you the sail number an' you can phone the boat people yourself if you like. No secret about that – it's going in the *Echo* tomorrow. But I've not had word myself on the owner an' I won't get it till that police girl comes back on duty; but when she picks up her messages from the dinghy people she'll know whose door to knock on...'

'An' they'll give me that door an' all, will they? The dinghy people? If I ring 'em?"

'Should do – 'less it's kept confidential. Mirrors list their sail numbers by years of manufacture. You quote the number at 'em an' they're supposed to tell you how old the boat is 'case you're thinking of buying one secondhand. That's the general scheme, according to my information.'

'Good. Then that'll do me, boy. An' if I don't get any joy off Mirrors I'll come back an' see you again. 'Cos I wanna be a jump ahead of the police, if you get me.' The silvery haired man started backing out. 'She's my daughter, my business, an' only mine.'

'Yeah, I get you.' And Charlie Gull started breathing more freely. And he did get the man; he understood all right. This big bloke would be back if he didn't get satisfaction down the phone. 'I'll give you the number off the sail,' he said. But his hand was shaking a bit for writing it down; and the man, when he heard it, said he'd remember it anyway. Loving fathers making do without their daughters don't forget crucial things like that.

Tom knocked the V for victory on the emergency exit door and Danni came to let him in. She hugged him, held his face hard in her hands and kissed him, deliberately on the lips. Just, 'Tom!' she said.

'Good news!' he told her. 'The silver eagle's back – and we might have some help.'

'Where?' She was looking at his hands for the necklace.

'Outside. The eagle, and the chance of some help...'

Danni looked over his shoulder, seemed to be seeing nothing, so Tom turned and called 'Phil!' in a low voice. And he held Danni firm and steady as Philip Swain came into view, already offering the eagle on the palm of his hand.

'I see you!' Danni reached out and snatched it, untangled the chain and strung it around her neck. Only when that was done did she scowl at Philip Swain. 'You take!' she accused him. 'Srać!'

Philip Swain put up his palms in admission. 'Yeah, I took it,' he repeated. 'But not off you, not in my head. I thought it belonged to the actors, in the play... I was going to return it to them.'

Danni was still scowling. 'Huh!' she snapped, and she flicked her fingers at him with a crack. 'Why you think this?'

Philip walked on up the steps at the side of the stage onto the set of *Flare Path*. 'Because it's...just like...' He sat on the edge of the hotel table. 'This was a play about wartime. Like the war it had a Polish airman in it, flying with the RAF. Their emblem was the eagle, their "wings". It's in one of the photographs.' He pointed to a picture at the foot of the hotel stairs. 'The Polish airman's wife wore that replica around her neck. She kept kissing it.'

Danni shook her head violently. 'Not this,' she said. 'Is mine!'

Tom looked at her and he felt like honey inside; she didn't treat Tom Robinson Welton like that; he was special to her. He went up onto the stage and looked at the framed photograph at the foot of the stairs. It showed a group of airmen, 218 squadron in front of a bomber, the crew of wartime fighters posing for the camera. Above the head of a smiling man in a roll necked sweater was the eagle Philip had seen, inset in gold.

'Yeah, air force eagle,' Tom said. 'It's the same, Dan.'

'So?'

'Somerthorpe had an RAF airfield, up in the beet fields. It's part of my project. Watson still uses a bit of the old runway as a road.' Tom looked at her, clicked his own fingers at her the way she clicked her fingers herself. 'You're Polish. Your eagle's the same as in the picture, Polish air force. They flew with us here in England – and what are we looking for? A place in England, round here! Strewth! I might have stuff about these Polish airmen, it might have been under my nose all the time!'

'If only you'd bashed the books harder,' said Philip Swain. 'Go on, then, Tom – go and see what you've got.'

Tom looked at the other two. 'In a minute,' he said. Because, excited as he was, he wasn't leaving Danni alone with Philip Swain, her feelings were still running strong about him taking her eagle. And she was Tom's responsibility. Swain had cocked things up before, he wasn't going to cock things up again. He might be bright in the books and learning sense but he was a bit of a dozo in real life.

'I'll go when Emma comes,' he said.

Tom spread out his project stuff on the settee in the front room. The maps of Somerthorpe from different ages he didn't need, but one of the books from the history section of the school library he had open at the index. It was 'East Anglia Airfields in the Second World War'. Was there any stuff about Polish airmen in there?

First he had to see if the word 'Polish' was in the index. And even with his iffy reading he could see that it wasn't; there was hardly a 'p' to be had. He blew out his cheeks. Perhaps they were stationed miles away, the Polish airmen, not East Anglia at all. Bugger! He shut the book, ready to pack it in. It looked like he'd have to go back to Danni with a nil result.

'That's my special boy. Up and at your work on a murky day.'

Tom looked up. His mum did try, she did encourage. She must have had a hard time at school, too, he reckoned.

'Made you some brain fodder.' She put a plateful of

toast down on the floor next to him.

'Thanks.'

'Cup o' tea?'

'Yeah, ta.'

Tom went back to the book. The student, the researcher – just for a minute, just for his mum. He took a bite of toast and flipped to the index on the off chance he'd missed 'Polish' the first time; but hard as he looked it still wasn't there. Last token effort – what about in the titles of chapters? But it wasn't there, either; just the airfields all listed and mapped.

'Two sugars for energy.' Here came the cup of tea.

'Ta.'

'PK – used to be nuts when I was a girl...'

'You're still weird now...'

'No, the letters.'

'What letters?'

'On the plane.' Tom's mum had picked up the airfield book and was looking at the Mustang on the cover, trying to show an interest, keeping him at it, pointing at the identification letters painted on the aircraft's side.

'They've all got those,' Tom said. He had looked at *some* of his project, he'd shown the flag. 'They identify their squadron.'

'Oh, yes?' But she didn't really care, she was only doing her mum duty. 'So, what squadron's PK, then?'

she asked, putting the book down and going back to the kitchen to flap at burnt toast.

'Dunno.'

'Don't matter, just asking…'

'Hold on!' And a sudden freeze had iced Tom's face; a fleeting touch of a brain-cold thought. PK! The airmen in the picture on the church-hall stage had a fighter plane behind them with *HA* painted on it – it had jumped out at him because the letters could have been the start of 'Harry'. Two letters again. So if *PK* and *HA* – what about *RF*, the letters on Danni's paper, would they fit, could they have been on the side of a plane? IDs all ran in patterns: cars had letters, numbers, and letters; fishing boats had harbour letters and numbers; Mirror dinghies were in strings of five numbers; and these RAF planes all seemed to have two main letters.

Was that it? Tom turned to the inside of the front cover, found the caption to the picture. And sounding it out, there was *Mustang* and there, too, was *squadron*.

And in the caption was another pattern – a pattern of three numbers. *A Mustang of 315 Squadron,* it said.

And Tom's mum came rushing back at the sight of Tom suddenly dancing around his plate of toast.

'Yes! Yes! Yes! Yes! *Yes!!*'

'So you're pleased about something, boy?'

'I am! I am!'

'And I knew you could do it; I knew, I knew.' Were those tears in her eyes?

Whatever, there was joy in Tom's. Tom Robinson Welton had cracked the code! Hadn't he just cracked the code? On the church-hall stage the picture had said 218 Squadron with *HA* painted on the plane's side. So what about *RF* – was that a squadron, too? And might that squadron be 303 by any chance? Tom scooped up the airfield book again – because just before the index at the back there had been a page of numbers. He found it, headed 'RAF Squadrons' – and underneath there were two columns, *Squadron* and *Page*. His finger danced a bee's flight down the lines. And he found it. He found it! 303. There it was, sweet! And next to it, the page number, 74. And there – turn the pages fast – was a picture of a Spitfire in flight; the eagle of the English sky; and painted on its soaring side were the squadron ID letters – *RF!*

'*Yes!*'

Danni's *RF 303* was no postcode, no car reg, no map reference. It was the squadron in which someone from Danni's family had flown back in the war.

'Oh, yes!' Tom shouted.

'Could you keep that noise down?' his father called at him from upstairs.

Tom didn't hear; because he was right into this, he was actually enjoying this, riding on the back of a bit of success. Plus he had a purpose, a crucial reason for doing it. He *needed* to find out. For Danni. What a cracking project to have!

He flipped to the back of the book and he saw the sticker of the bookshop where it had been bought by the school. The RAF Museum, Hendon. He had trouble with reading *museum* but none with running to the hall, dialling 192 and getting put through – while his father came downstairs and ate Tom's toast muttering something about keeping lines clear in case of emergency.

The bookshop assistant at Hendon passed Tom to the Research and Information department. Tom was connected. 'I'm doing some research on 303 squadron in the Second World War,' he went on; 'and I need to know, did it have a Polish airman in it, and could you tell me where it flew from, what airfield?'

The man knew straight off. 'It wasn't one airman who was Polish, 303 was an all Polish outfit. And like most other squadrons, it didn't fly from one airfield – it flew from various, different parts of the UK, earned a magnificent reputation, too.'

'Oh, so they went all over the place?'

'A handful of stations – but it had its most famous days at RAF Coltishall. Virtually finished up there...'

'Coltishall,' Tom repeated. He took a significant breath. 'And where's that, please?' He was praying that Coltishall wasn't in the north of Scotland.

'Norfolk,' the man said. 'Just north of Norwich…'

And Tom wanted to jump again, and sing, and twirl the cord of the phone around him in a wiggly snake dance. But researchers don't do that, not with fathers scowling at them. Instead, as he clicked his fingers at his mum to pass him a ballpoint, he asked down the phone how you spelt Coltishall.

'What's with all this blessed Polish stuff?' his dad called after him as Tom stuffed the spelling in his top pocket and ran for the front door.

But he got no answer. Tom was on his way. He headed along the small terrace towards the junction with Glebe Lane. He ran past a car parked up outside the house a few doors down, a passing look to see who was in it, someone with a plaster on his cheek just looking up from a street map –

– And *no!* It was Harry – looking hatchet spiteful.

Tom wanted to yell but he hadn't got a voice. He wanted to run but his legs seemed to have lost their strength. He wanted to turn back to the house but the car was in the way.

Harry! That spiteful bullying abuser!

And from flying high, chasing the clouds in the glint of the sun, Tom was suddenly nose-diving to the earth. Shot down. Wiped out.

Killed in action.

CHAPTER SIXTEEN

Oh, God!

In the middle of the junction Tom suddenly swerved away from Glebe Lane, sprinted a diagonal down towards the town – forget the church hall, he mustn't lead the man there! Behind him came the wild rev of an engine and the squeal of tyres as Tom ran for his life. How did the man know? They must have got his dinghy number, knew who'd rescued Danni, and Charlie Gull had told this monster where he lived. And Tom knew too much! The man had heard Danni shout it out, he knew she'd have told him. If he caught Tom he'd kill him to shut him up! He'd be an accident they'd find in the sea – after he'd been tortured to tell where Danni was. Bad torture because he'd never do that, he'd die first! But he had a fighting chance if he could get down into the town; he couldn't be snatched off a pavement full of holidaymakers, could he?

Tom pelted on, but there was a hell of a way to go. The road was thick hedged on both sides so there was nowhere to run but straight on. And the car had turned, it was coming down behind him. He didn't know he could run so fast. His legs pumped and his trainers hit the road hard enough to hurt. There was no ditch to dive in and there were a hundred metres to go before the road dropped into the top end of Somerthorpe – so he had *no* chance! The car was coming closer – and the man *would* run him down, cripple him; he was a bully and he wanted Danni back to do more of the same.

But Tom wasn't giving in till he was forced to, he went pounding on, the car on top of him now; a hopeless run about to be cut short any second! Scare seared inside him as he braced himself for the crunch. How much would it hurt? How mangled would his legs be?

When around the bend from the town came the Lowestoft bus, its diesel clattering up the hill. In view – and nothing for it, Tom took the last and biggest chance of his life, the only thing he could do: he ran out in front of the car. *Brake or kill! Stop or hit me!* And the man stopped with shrieking tyres to mark the road for five years as Tom raced across and threw out his hand to halt the bus. And to looks from the jolted passengers that said everything about stupid kids, Tom got on the vehicle that had just been shocked rigid into stopping.

'Better I don' tell your dad, boy,' the driver said.

'Ta.' Tom paid his fare, all the way, and sat on an aisle seat trying not to snort as he heaved for breath. He looked around at the road behind; where Harry was turning the car again to follow. But Tom wasn't too worried about that, not for now. He'd got some space, he'd saved himself, he hadn't been run down, and he was taking Harry away from Danni; the man might even think she was still hiding up in Lowestoft. At last he got his breath back, his heart went back to thumping a bit nearer to normal. Well, he couldn't be got at with people around, could he? And he reckoned he could lose Harry once they were in the town in a bus lane where the car couldn't follow. He'd get off – or not get off – at the busiest bus stop with all the others, and by the time Harry was out of his car he'd lose himself in the holiday crowds.

And – bonus thought – he could get his bike back. The only thing he couldn't do was go back home; not until he'd sorted Danni. So he sat on the bus and bided his time, checking behind on the road every few minutes. And when they reached the traffic of Lowestoft the bus lost Harry at lights and soon Tom was running again, for his bike...

*

Danni was in fresh clothes. Emma had decided she'd help. When Tom came back to the church hall and knocked his V for victory on the emergency exit Danni let him in wearing new stuff, things he'd seen on Emma. And she looked good – a new twist, Danni in an Emma Thorpe summer top and shorts, with the silver eagle sparkling round her neck again. Instead of her red headscarf she was in a floppy summer beanie and from beneath it, head on one side, her teeth sparkled in a smile that asked, 'What do you reckon?'

Tom kissed her. It just felt natural, like two French exchange kids, except their kiss was on the lips.

'Long time you been. You find things?'

'I've found Harry—'

'Srać!' A sudden dark cloud.

'He was outside my house but I got away and took him to Lowestoft – it's all right, he's miles off.'

Danni made the sign of the cross.

'I've found my bike, and, yup, I've found things.' Tom pushed his bike in and wheeled it to the main hall where Emma and Philip were waiting. '…I've found the code,' he said proudly. 'Cracked it. *RF 303.*'

'Which is?' Philip asked, as if cracking codes was everyday.

'Was. 303 was a Polish squadron of the RAF, flew from Coltishall…'

'Norwich!' Emma said.

'Not far, too! And it fits.'

'Please? This is what?' Danni was impatient, she whip-cracked her hand in wanting to know.

'Your great-grandfather – or uncle – if he wrote that address you've got, there's a chance he could have been a Polish airman at Coltishall. RF was the code on their planes, 303 was their squadron number. *RF 303,* see? And if his family lives at the White House, or in a white house near there – we've found them!'

Tom's eyes were bright at Danni, who suddenly screamed into his face, 'You are beautiful!' And she grabbed him and rocked him and hugged him and kissed him, hard.

'Yeah, well done,' said Philip. 'Congratulations.'

'Sure. Great!' said Emma in a new sounding voice. 'Excellent result!'

'I'll get you my OS map of the area,' Philip Swain said. 'You can take your bikes on the train from Ipswich to Norwich. Then head north.'

'I'll get my bike,' Emma said to Danni, 'and you two can get off.' And without looking again at Tom she left the hall.

'*Perhaps* I've found them. Only *perhaps,*' Tom was saying.

'"Perhaps" better than "not". So we go, find my family…' When suddenly the happy Danni turned on

Philip Swain. 'You say sorry for eagle?' she demanded.

'I thought I had.'

'Strewth, thought Tom, if she liked you she liked you. If she didn't, listen to this...

'You make bad for me, you make bad for Tom, you creep in like man who want to catch and hurt, you make me run...'

But Philip Swain wasn't taking that. His eyes were big with outrage, his skin had gone milk pale and his voice was sinister calm. 'Don't ever call me that! Don't ever think you're the only one that stuff has happened to!'

'What you mean?' Danni's arms were folded.

He looked at her as if he might say more; but, suddenly, 'Never mind. I'll get that map.' And with a quick look at Tom, Philip Swain walked out of the hall.

Danni shrugged. 'What he mean?'

'Dunno,' said Tom. It could have been being an orphan; it could have been being mistreated, beaten like her. Tom didn't want to talk about it; but, thinking about it, Swain *was* fostered to the Thorpes for some good reason; there was more to him than anyone ever said. Maybe Tom Robinson Welton, who'd always thought he was rungs down on the ladder, had always been rungs up – at least as far as having a normal family went. Who knew?

'So we go, find family.'

'Yup, we go, find your family. But we take great care – that Harry mustn't find us first. We'll be on bikes but he can cover ground fast in his car...'

Danni was smiling, head up and proud. 'But not run quick – ' she said '– with bad leg.'

Coming back to the house for his midday break George Welton stopped and frowned. There was a car outside his house with people sitting in it. Two of them. He went over to it.

'Can I help you?'

'Eh?' The man in the driving seat looked up at him, a silvery haired older man. Next to him was a big woman with black dyed hair.

'Don't know you, do I? Around here?' George Welton's coastguard shirt was Persil white and his voice was starched. 'You sitting outside my house for a reason?'

'I am as it goes, boy.' The man got out of the car. He had a fraying plaster on his cheek, just under the right eye. 'I think I owe your son a vote of thanks.'

'Yeah? What for?'

'Saving my girl from the sea. My daughter.'

'*Your* daughter?'

'Danuta.'

'Polish, is that?' George Welton's eyes weren't blinking.

'Well, step-daughter. He took her off them rocks you've got out there. In his Mirror boat.'

George Welton folded his arms. 'Yeah, I just heard that. Bit of a mystery all round. He don't say much…'

'No mystery, boy. She's had a row wi' me, father an' kid stuff, an' she's run off – an' now she's too scared to come home…'

'To Coltishall?'

'Coltishall?' The man's axe edge of a face had sharpened some. 'Is that what she said?'

'I don't know anything she's said,' George Welton replied. 'Haven't seen her myself, it's what *he* said…'

'But you reckon that's where she's headed?'

George Welton unfolded his arms. 'Heard the place dropped out in talk, that's all. Were you once RAF?'

'No, boy, didn't do National Service.'

'You're not from Coltishall, then?'

'Lowestoft.'

'An' you're English?'

'More'n the Queen. Pure blood. So's my sister.' He waved a hand at the woman in the car who was staring out through the windscreen.

George Welton scratched at his cheek. 'Well I don't understand it. Do you want to come back later? We can both have a word with my boy…'

But the man was shaking his head, getting back into his car. 'I'll see how I go,' he said. 'You might have give me what I need to know…'

'Yes?' George Welton went to his gate. 'Well remember I'm his father. You're her father, I'm his. He answers to me, not to no one else.'

'He'll answer where it's due!' The man slammed his car door and drove off. Northwards. As George Welton watched him out of sight.

Tom and Danni wheeled their bikes off the train at Norwich, came out of the station and looked for a road sign to take them to the B1150. There was nothing straight off, but Tom was good on maps, he could read Ordnance Survey signs and symbols better than most. Resting on their saddles, he and Danni checked on the sheet.

'We go up here and we come to the ring road,' Tom said.

Danni leant over, steadied herself with a hand on his shoulder; normal, natural; his shoulder was hers to lean on without asking. 'To A147,' she said, and her finger touched his on the map: small contact, still big thrill. 'Then B1150.' She looked across at the street sign, the name of the first leg. She spelt it out. 'Ri-ver-side Road.'

'That's it. Riverside. Up here then across the ring road and north west to Coltishall.'

'So why we wait?' Her voice was demanding but

she was smiling under her beanie hat; and in her summer clothes on Emma's bike she flipped Tom again.

'Yeah, why?' And Tom pushed off, up the road. They rode fast and were at the A147 and turning right at the roundabout onto the B1150 within ten minutes. 'This is it,' Tom said over his shoulder in their single file, 'all the way home now...'

'Hope!' said Danni. 'Hope is home!'

But as they crossed the north Norwich ring road at New Sprowston a car was coming to the same roundabout – a blue Ford Mondeo with a hot, silver haired man hunched over its steering wheel, a big staring woman next to him. As any trucker knew, the A1042 ring road was notorious for its crawl and the Ford was in the slow nearside lane. The man looked up. Suddenly he swore; his face twisted and he punched the woman's shoulder – because there with the boy he'd chased was a girl whose face was hidden in the shadow of a floppy hat.

'Little clat! There she is!' And he cursed God out of his heaven as the Mondeo missed its lane for a right turn onto the B1150 – it would have to go on to the next roundabout at the A140 junction and come back. Unless he took the A140 north and cut across country to Coltishall; both roads led to the airfield. 'We can still bloody get there first!' the man said to the woman.

'You'd better had, boy!' she replied. 'Now the mother's gone…' And she laughed a spiteful laugh.

Up the B1150 was a longish push for Tom and Danni. At half past two they stopped for a cola and a Mars bar at a roadside shop near a church. The sun had come out and they sat in the shade of a beech tree catching their breaths. But Tom couldn't sit still for long; nothing would be settled till Danni had found out about her father's great-uncle from the RAF people, till they knew whether he was still alive or not, and they found out what had happened to his family. Restlessly, he wandered between the graves as he tore the wrapper off his Mars bar. He was tense, impatient – and yet somehow he didn't want this over. He feared finding out the worst – there'd be no old airman, no family, because what would happen then, for real – hadn't his adoption talk been a bit glib?

And there it was staring at him. From a grave. There was that same swooping eagle Danni had around her neck, carved into a headstone: and beneath it was chiselled a name, a long name, and Tom knew it wasn't English.

'Dan! Look! Over here!'

'What?'

Tom pointed to the headstone.

'"*Stanislaw Raczkiewicz*",' she read out. '"*1922-*

1998. I have fought a good fight. I have finished my course. I have kept the faith."' She turned to look at Tom. 'Airman. Polish,' she said quietly. 'Die here.'

'But not your family?'

She shook her head.

'It means they're around, though! We're on the right course!'

She gripped his arm fiercely. 'We hope, yes?'

'We hope!' Tom said as they ran back for their bikes.

CHAPTER SEVENTEEN

The Senior Aircraftsman on guard duty at the gates of RAF Coltishall watched the blue Ford Mondeo as it passed in front of him. It was the third pass it had made. They got a lot of aircraft enthusiasts out here to see the Jaguars on their training flights but mostly they waited with their cameras on the other side of the airfield, nearer the runway. Behind the airman was the Guard Room and further through the Operations Buildings. Across the road in front of the gates were acres of flat fields broken by lines of old pollarded trees. As the car came past again, the man in it was looking in hard through the gates, the woman staring ahead like a spotter's bored wife. Or she could be an accomplice acting innocent? The airman fingered the trigger of his slung submachine gun. There wasn't a black alert on, but terrorism was in the air. On the other hand the pair of them could just be looking out for an airman they knew.

The car came past again and parked up. The man

got out – white, male, late fifties or sixties, silver hair, staring fish eyes.

'Any kids been round here?' the man asked.

'Plenty, sir. No school. Holidays, isn't it?'

'On bikes?'

'Bikes, rollerblades, skateboards – you name it. They live here.' The airman pointed to the roads of houses that made up a big, active fighter station.

'No older kids, strangers…?'

'I don't know 'em all.' The airman pointed in through the gate to the nearer buildings. 'You want the Guard Room or the Orderly Room,' he said. 'Ask there if you like.'

'Girl in a hat, boy with dark hair?'

'Can't say. You'll have to ask in there.'

The man seemed to think about it. He fiddled with a plaster on his cheek. 'Well, thanks for nothing!' And he went back to his car.

Now the airman on guard duty did make a mental note of the Mondeo's number plate as it drove away. Just in case.

It was nearly too late when Danni saw it. But it's hard to hide up a car in the flatness of East Anglia, and Harry was a trucker, not SAS and trained in camouflage. The Mondeo was at the side of the road ahead of them, in a lay-by. Right at that moment Tom was somewhere else in his head – as they cycled the road to the airfield he'd been looking from side to side at every house on the search for a 'White House' sign, or just a big white house.

'*Srác! Harry!*' Danni shouted, suddenly swerving onto a verge and pulling Tom with her. They fell off together in a spoky tangle.

'Harry? Where?' Tom was on his knees, head up, alert.

'There! Car! This car I know!'

'What's its reg?'

'Uh?'

'Don't look.' He twisted her head to him. 'Look at me and tell me its number plate.'

Danni understood. 'L294FJH,' she said into his eyes, hard to hear in the roar of two Jaguar fighters making a low pass across the fields.

Tom checked with the vehicle up ahead. 'That's the one! The sod! How's he got here?'

'Some traitor? That boy?'

Tom shrugged. He didn't know; but, 'Not Swain,' he said.

'So – what we do? He is king of this road there!'

Tom looked along at the car in the lay-by, and all around. It was true, there was no getting past it. And the Mondeo was facing away from them – so however fast they cycled past, it would be after them pronto without having to make a turn. But right now nothing was moving about the car, no door was inching open; the driver would have to be looking into his rear view mirror all the time to pick up everything going on behind him; and Tom reckoned he and Danni were lucky, they hadn't been seen. Yet.

'The map.' Tom pulled their bikes tighter into the hedge at the side of the verge and unfolded Philip Swain's OS sheet. He looked up and around for landmarks. 'Church, there,' he said, 'behind us.' And he found it on the map. *'Rems.'*

'Rems? Is what?'

'Remains – old, knocked down…' And sure enough what they could see of the building was in ruins. 'Which means we're right here.' He put his finger on the map's orange-coloured road. 'And he's up there, on that clear stretch.'

'So we need getting…?' The Jaguar aircraft roared above them again, the afterburn of their engines shaking the ground.

'There, look – see the dotted line of the runway?' Tom found the airfield; it was the same as on the wartime map of Somerthorpe. 'We're heading there.'

Danni sat back on her heels. 'And he is there. Between.' And she whip-cracked her fingers impatiently.

Her knees shone in the sun as Tom went back to

the map. 'Let's have a look.' His finger traced it again – and he just had to grip one of those smooth knees in triumph when he found what he wanted. A chance. 'Look – here.' To the right of the road they were on, on the airfield side, was a long black line running between series of black shadings which looked like centipedes on the paper. 'Railway,' Tom said, 'but can you see it? In real life?'

Danni looked about her. 'No railway,' she said – and ducked as a third Jaguar fighter roared overhead. 'Airplane. Not railway.'

'But there is, look.' Tom took her attention down to the map. 'What's that say, printed along that line?'

'"Bu-re Vall-ey Rail-way",' Danni read.

'Right – well, that's summer tourist stuff, miniature, Bure Valley. And see here – these loads of little black marks on either side of the line, they tell us either "embankment" or "cutting". And where there's none the railway's on the surface...'

'So?'

'Well, these here, *these* little black marks,' he pointed to the marks nearest to their position, 'they're thick on the outside and they get thinner – that's a cutting; and these ones up the road, they're thick on the inside and going out thinner – that's an embankment. Up high.'

'How you know this?'

Tom said it without looking up, he was too engrossed. 'I can read maps, you learn these symbols. Now – if we go back to this little cross, that's a proper church, not rems, we go over the road and head along the side of this field past these woods...' His finger showed where a boundary line on the map went by a little green box of tree symbols. 'And when we get to the railway, this bit of track up past that Mondeo is down in the cutting. So Harry can look across the fields as hard as he likes and if he doesn't know the railway's there he won't see us going by.'

'Clever!' Danni whispered. 'Clever Tom!'

Tom pretended he hadn't heard. 'We come up from the cutting here – and we follow that dead-end lane to this radio mast...' He looked up from the symbol on the map and pointed to the real thing in the distance. 'Then it's along the edge of that field, up through that little estate, and there's the way into the airfield.'

Danni looked at him hard. 'So we jump in plane and fly to Poland! Be good!'

It took him a moment to latch on to what she said. 'Yeah, be good, me and you.' He smiled at her. 'No, we do what we've come for, we go to the people there and ask about the Polish 303 squadron. They were famous here so if anyone knows about them, they will. Please God.'

'Sure. Please God.' Danni was getting up. 'So, what

we wait for, clever man?'

'Nothing. We hide our bikes in the rems of this church – and we go.'

'We go!'

And following the map, along past the wood and slithering down a barren bank, they crouched and ran to a deep and empty railway cutting with shining narrow-gauge rails.

'It's in use,' Tom said. 'See? Not rusty. Keep listening, and no talking.' Tom knew too well that things could suddenly go wrong. Twice already Harry had jumped them both, and once he'd jumped him; Harry was the sort who could have his ear to the ground and would suddenly rear up above them at the cutting's top. So they made it as fast as they could along Tom's route, stopping only to check the map against the terrain or to wait and listen till a Jaguar had roared across in case it was masking the sound of a car on the move; and they turned no corner, ran across no stretch, skirted no field without waiting like trained saboteurs to make sure the coast was clear before committing themselves. And there were no trains; they heard a steamy whistle in the distance but by then, blowing in relief, they were running through the married quarters and coming to the gates of RAF Coltishall. Drawing breath, they walked up to the airman on guard duty.

'No bikes?' he said – but he said nothing about a Mondeo as he directed them to the Guard Room where visitors had to report.

Ten minutes later, Warrant Officer Warrender came to the desk, summoned by the civilian on duty – and it took just one look at the silver eagle around Danni's neck for him to be doing a little stamp of a dance.

'Sweetheart jewellery! I didn't know the Poles had it.' In no time he had taken them over to his office. 'This is really exciting, young lady.' All the way across the neat pathways he hadn't been able to take his eyes off the necklace.

'Sweetheart jewellery?' Tom got to ask as he sat them down.

'Copies. Wartime replicas of service badges for wives and sweethearts. The RAF boys had them made up, their "wings", their "half wings" with their trade letters on them – "O" for Observer, "N" for Navigator, that sort of thing. Their better halves wore them with pride, and for luck. But I've never seen a Polish one…'

'Not here, sweethearts?' Danni asked.

'You are joking!' said WO Warrender.

'Well, that's why we're here,' Tom went on. 'We're looking for one of Danuta's old great-uncles who sent this eagle back to Poland, but we're not sure when. He might be alive, he might be dead. We think he stayed on after the war. We hope.'

The officer was nodding. He was a smallish man with sleek black gelled hair and round librarian glasses. Now he was washing his hands vigorously without soap or water. 'The reason the girl at the desk called me was because for my sins I run the History Room. What's his name, your relative?' He was halfway into his desk drawer already.

'Mikawski,' said Danni. 'Bronislau Mikawski.'

And they both jumped as the WO slapped his hand flat onto the desk like a teacher waking up a class.

'Orzel Mikawski!' he almost squeaked. '*Orzel!*'

'No, Bronislau,' said Tom.

'Yes, I know – but that was his nickname in the squadron. Orzel!'

'Says eagle,' Danni said simply.

'I'll say. He hunted like the eagle, already before he came here from Northolt he was an ace. He was a real one-off like a lot of the Poles, slow to take orders if they didn't suit, quick to take a chance and chase a Messerschmitt, even into clouds...'

'A hero?' Tom asked, looking at Danni.

'Hero indeed. And here's the news you want to hear...' Because Danni's expression hadn't changed; her eyes were wide and her mouth was open as she clutched her silver eagle in tight fingers: waiting to be told something vitally important to her future. He slowed and lowered his voice. 'Orzel lived through the war. He married a local girl, stayed on in the RAF for a bit, flew commercial stuff out of Norwich for a few years while his family grew up. And...' Even a disciplined RAF WO couldn't hold off from a moment's dramatic suspense. '– he's still alive. His son bought a pub, a granddaughter runs it now. And he's still a character, a bit of a legend – and you should get in the White Horse some Saturday nights with a few of our Jaguar boys...'

'The White *Horse*?' Tom asked.

'The White Horse: a pub, half a mile or so down the road at Little Hautbois. That's where he lives, great old man – but don't ever cross him!'

Tom was shaking his head. 'Not the White *House* or anything?'

'No, the White Horse.'

Tom looked at Danni who was already clutching his hand. 'His writing's as bad as mine, then!' he said.

'So how to find this White Horse?' she was asking.

'Back down the road. Where it does a sharp left, just by the tourist railway, that corner, there's your White Horse.'

'Could you show me on the map?' Tom asked. WO Warrender did so. And Tom read it now from the symbol, a blue half-filled tankard – public house. 'Thanks!'

'No problem! And good luck! Give Orzel my best.'

But already Tom was folding the map and he and Danni were halfway out of the door.

Meanwhile, Harry was on his mobile phone.

'That the RAF?'

'RAF Coltishall,' the operator replied.

'Guard Room,' he demanded. And after several clicks he was put through.

It was back to the map again, and the tourist railway cutting. Left of the main gate Tom and Danni slipped through the married quarters, past the school, and back across the field by the radio mast. Their eyes were everywhere, because Harry was about. As he read the map, Tom realised that they must have passed the White Horse pub on their way to the airfield but they'd been down in the cutting and so hadn't seen it up on the surface.

'Don't believe! Don't believe!' Danni kept saying. In all her alertness sometimes she squeezed his hand, sometimes she clapped him on the back, once she kissed him on the cheek as they stopped to check direction. 'Is here! Is alive! We find what Matka want.'

'Nearly, we have, nearly,' Tom said. 'Come on, let's get there quick and do the business...'

'"*Business*?" Is my *life*!'

'Come on!' And they ran the railway track between the steep sides of the cutting, Tom counting paces as they went. But this time it wasn't going to be the easy job they'd had before. Like sailing, if the wind's with you one way it's against you going back. The Jaguars had roared in, one, two, three and landed; the whole countryside seemed very still. And very audible now came the first sounds of trouble – the pinging of the cable running beside the railway track. A signal up ahead was being changed; and seconds later the track took on a hum – which meant that a train was coming! OK, the cutting was wide enough to let it pass – but what if it stopped? What if trespassers on the track made the driver halt his engine and cause a commotion? The last thing Tom wanted was to have to climb the cutting's side and show out on top.

Now the humming became a rumbling and there was that steamy whistle they'd heard before, but nearer, a lot nearer. What to do? Where to go? The cutting side was bare, there was nowhere to hide down here. But fifty metres up ahead was a bridge which had to be spanning the road.

'Quick, Dan! Bridge! Get behind it!' Tom led the run, hard and fast along between the lines now, ducking when he got to the low bridge; and just seconds before the train came around the last bend, they both threw themselves behind the brickwork. To passengers facing backwards they'd look like terrorists flattened there, but the driver wouldn't have seen them.

The train came on past, not very fast. An engine was pulling five covered carriages, the driver sitting there stoking with a small shovel like a big kid at a fête. And cramped in the little seats were holidaymakers, bored stiff with being in a cutting.

The train went on, just a couple of kids pointing, adults staring; but what was that Tom could suddenly hear above them, coming to the bridge? It was a car on the road. Which could have been one of a million – but which could also be Harry on a patrol. And was it slowing down? Oh God, it was – Tom heard the rub of brake linings.

Danni had frozen. 'I know that! Mondeo! She squeak!' She pulled Tom with her under the arch of the bridge as a car door slammed. Breathing stopped, Tom's legs twitched in spasm as he shut his eyes to hear better – those footsteps on the road above; one heavy, one lighter with a bit of drag; someone with a limp.

It *was* Harry! No doubt, it *was* Harry – and right now he was within metres of the girl he wanted to grab back...

CHAPTER EIGHTEEN

The man was scarier than ever because he couldn't be seen, just imagined. What had he got in his hand; the spanner, a knife, a *gun*? What had he got in his evil head? Tom grabbed at Danni's hand and they squeezed each other till it should have hurt; but like two preyed-upon animals they were in a fight-to-survive state. What wouldn't the monster be ready to do to get his little slave back? He'd chased Danni like someone hungry for her – and right now he was only feet above them on the bridge. Tom could hear the rustle of his sleeve on the parapet as he leant on it, probably over it; he heard the man breathing; and he heard him cross to the other side of the road where he had to be looking up and down the track – and thank God for that train coming or he'd have seen them from the bridge.

It couldn't have been for more than thirty seconds, the double checking – but down below it seemed forever. Just as Tom's muscles wanted to shout, though, the limping footsteps could be heard again, the car door clicked quietly closed, more sinister than a slam, and the car's engine started, was jerked into gear and driven off.

But was Harry still in it? Tom was onto the man now, he could read his devious mind. Had he suspected something up there? Might the person with him have driven off and Harry was standing silent above, waiting for them to come out?

Tom put his finger to his lips, he shook his head in a warning to Danni to keep silent, not to move yet. He pointed his finger towards the surface; and he made them wait frozen like that, listening with ears tuned so sensitively that they could have picked up a butterfly's wings.

Nothing! But Tom couldn't take the chance. He looked at Danni, tense, scared, so near to getting to her goal. And he knew what he had to do.

'Stay here!' he hissed. 'I'm going up to check...'

Danni shook her head vigorously. 'Not!'

'I'm going up to check.' Whispered but firm. 'And if he's there I'm running like hell whatever way I can. Decoy. I'll make him come after me...'

'He has knife!'

'He has limp! But you – ' he pointed ahead along the track ' – you get down to that far bend. I reckon your pub should be somewhere up above.'

'Tom…'

'And take care!'

He put his finger to his own lips and to hers, to keep them both silent – but also in a sort of blessing, the way it had been in his shed.

But if that was a blessing Harry was the curse; right now he was the danger in their world. Tom could forget his feelings, he had to stay alive to feel anything! Stealthily, he came out from under the bridge and inched himself like a spy to climb to the road above. Any second he might see Harry – or hear Harry shout as the man came for him. Slowly, spider lightly, he climbed to where he could see but would also be seen, and holding his breath ready for the run, he put his head around the parapet; to see – nothing. No one. Harry had gone with the car.

Quickly, he slid back down the cutting to Danni, who was standing there with a fist to her mouth. 'All clear!' he said gruff and matter-of-fact. He looked at Danni's scared face: scared for him. He looked at her. She wasn't Emma Thorpe. Emma was pretty, every boy's dream, and she had everything. But Danni was something else: she had nothing, less than nothing, and she wasn't pretty in Emma's way – but she was surprising and exciting and a woman, and her Polish gypsy face was more than pretty, it was beautiful. And if they could dodge Harry and get to the White Horse there was a chance she'd stay in England and he wouldn't ever have to say goodbye to her.

'Come on!' He led the way on down the track towards the White Horse; and three minutes later – and correct according to the map and the distance he reckoned they'd covered – they came to a rickety flight of wooden steps leading up to the surface. 'It'll be about here,' Tom said. 'I'm going up to look.'

'Safe! You be safe!'

'Name of the game!' And Tom climbed the creaky steps. He came to the top, head down and as cautious as reconnaissance again, and there it was! The White Horse. He'd read the map dead accurately. There beside the cutting, well back from the road with its own car park out in front of it was the pub, its sign hanging proud on a thick black post, a white racehorse. There was a white van and a car parked outside – which wasn't a blue Mondeo; and wooden tables sitting empty in front of the long, red-brick building with its tall chimney stacks and one door into the bar.

Tom ran back to the steps to call Danni up. And it could almost have been in slow motion, the thoughts that filled his head in their short run across the car park. Yes, this was it, now was the time; his project – his special project – was nearly over. They'd dodged Harry, got here safely, and Danni had found her real family, please God. Now she could stay and be content with them.

But although he'd see her again – and he'd definitely see her again – never would they be holed up together, sharing the closeness, having the special private thing they'd had. So this, now, was their last moment, the end of what had begun when he'd rescued her off the rocks.

'Dan,' he said, her floppy hat hiding her beautiful face, 'whatever goes off from now on, good luck in your life!'

She looked at him and he could see that she was trembling. 'Tom,' she said, stroking his face, and he realised she said his name like no one else, she made it sound so special. If only she could say three other special words. But they kissed, a long, probing, trembling kiss in the yard of the White Horse: and together, holding hands, they walked in from the brightness to the gloom of the bar.

And to Harry the trucker.

A freezing, heart-stopping moment. Danni screamed at Tom as he turned back for the door – but the way out was suddenly blocked by a big black haired woman who'd come from somewhere behind it.

With a pint in his hand Harry was sitting at a dark shiny table, flicking the ash off a cigarette into a metal ashtray. A big man in a sweatshirt was standing by him and a woman was leaning over the bar, had to have been listening to something he was saying.

'You c'n come in, you two,' said Harry. 'Beat you to it.'

Tom spun back as Danni screamed again, but the bar was small inside and there was nowhere to run.

'All right, all right,' said the woman behind the bar, and she came around to put a hand on Danni's shoulder.

The big man in the sweatshirt had folded his arms and was frowning as Harry stayed smoking and supping like harmless old Captain Cat. 'So what's all this you're saying?'

'I'm saying this here's my daughter.'

'No! No! Not him! Not! Him, I hate!' Danni shrieked.

'She's Polish!' Tom shouted. 'She's not his, she don't belong to him!'

On the word 'Polish' the pub people looked hard at each other.

But, 'Oh, you took your time, boy.' Harry had turned to Tom, his eyes staring hate. 'The Air Force filled me in. I should be cross wi' you, running off with my girl. *My* girl, who I've come to love...' But it was said for the others, not for Tom.

'Yeah! We know your love!' Tom backed away from him. 'Are you Polish?' he asked the other man with a quick look round.

'Me? No. I'm her husband. Frank.' He nodded at the woman with Danni. 'She is, partly. We run this place. It's his.' He pointed to a painting above the fireplace; and dominating the bar was a portrait of a wartime airman, dark haired, dark eyed, staring into the room with intent. And Tom knew who that was: the eyes in the picture were Danni's eyes. It was Orzel, the Eagle: the wartime ace.

'The wife's grandfather.'

'Which means – ' Tom's voice was shaking, this was so important, ' – you won't know this, but that means that this girl, Danni, is her cousin. Or second, third cousin, or whatever. Danuta.' And his voice rose, firmer – 'And she's running away from him!' His face twisted as he pointed at Harry.

But all Harry was doing was shaking his head, a benevolent old man who wouldn't hurt a fly, looking as calm as anything, not moving a muscle as he followed Danni with his eyes while she scuttled the long way around the table to the man Frank and lifted the silver eagle on her necklace.

And with the special eagle in her fingers she suddenly showed no fear. All at once she was as proud as Tom had ever seen her, her face was lifted with it. She would have fought women, men, police, governments as a brave Polish gypsy. 'This, he sends, Orzel – to father, mine. Real father, Polski.' She pointed at the portrait. 'This man sends. He is – I think – great-grand-uncle.'

'What's your name?' the woman asked. 'Danni? Danuta – what?'

'Danuta Mikawski, me!'

'I'm Dorota Webb.' The woman had lowered her voice. 'Was Dorota Mikawski.'

'Same. Same family.'

'See? Same family!' Tom shouted. 'Your family!' He pointed at Harry. 'And this man's not!'

'I am, boy, I married her mother.' It was said as quiet and calm as an undertaker at a graveside.

'Not the right-hand ring, she only wore it on the left…' Tom had remembered. 'Opposite to the Polish way for real marrying.'

Dorota Mikawski cleared her throat, she was slowly nodding; she had rings on both hands.

Harry thumped down his beer glass and was standing up. 'I tell the lot of you, she's my family, and I'm taking her home. An' if you try and stop me, she's going for the police.' He waved a hand behind him at his sister by the door. 'This is a load of old bollocks. The girl got the wrong side of me, she's made up all sorts of lies she can't prove, and now I'm taking her home where she belongs.' He looked across the room at the man, Frank. 'And you try anything on, boy, you'll end up in Norwich jail. An' that's a promise, not a threat!' Said just as the sudden clump of a stick could be heard on the stairs.

'Hold on!' said Frank. 'Not so fast.'

Harry stopped as everyone turned to the stairs – to watch as stick-first, someone came down into the bar. He was old, he was bald, but he was tall and proud. Tom stared at him hard. From those dark eyes there was no doubt in his mind who this was. He was the man in the picture. He was Orzel the fighter pilot; and the bar changed, instantly – his presence altered the whole atmosphere.

'We ain't got time,' Harry's sister said.

But, 'What's this?' Orzel was demanding. 'The screaming and the shouting? A man can't sleep in the afternoon, is that it?' He was addressing the woman at the bar.

Harry watched like a lynx as Frank Webb led Danni over to the old man.

'You want to see this,' he told him, and pointed to the eagle around Danni's neck.

'Trinket,' Harry said.

'Knick-knack,' said his sister.

But old Bronislau, Orzel, was focusing his sharp eyes on Danni. He took the eagle in his fingers, lifted it and held it close with Danni having to move nearer. He said nothing, looked at the eagle – and showed nothing on his face.

'You are?' he finally asked, keeping her there as he held the silver bird.

'Danuta Mikawski.'

'She's Danuta Smith! My daughter!' Harry picked up a chair and thumped it down. 'I tell you, this is a load of old bollocks – she's my daughter and I've come to take her home where she belongs. Eagle! Bloody eagle! I've heard enough of all this crap! Come here!' He made a grab towards Danni, but Orzel suddenly raised his walking stick and held him off – the way Tom had first raised his stick at the docks.

'Hold on! Where's your hurry?'

Harry took a pace back, looked around at his sister who was still at the door. The old pilot's gaze went back to Danni and the silver necklace, which he squinted and stared at like a jeweller making a valuation. He breathed in and out quietly, and at last he spoke; softly, very softly. 'Family! *Family!*' His voice was shaking now. 'For Evelyn it was made, and when she died, I sent it home, home to Warszawa. But, no word.' He shrugged. 'Many years ago. Everyone is dead, I'm thinking. All Mikawskis like all old Poland is dead. But, no.' His voice suddenly strengthened and he gripped Danni's shoulders hard. 'And this man – ' he was looking at Harry ' – he is…?'

'Legally…' Dorota put in.

'I keep telling everyone, I'm the girl's father,' Harry

shouted. 'I married her mother and now she's Danuta Smith, step-daughter of Harry Smith, legal, and you can let her go and I take her home or my sister's going for the police.'

'She's teenage,' the sister came in, low and croaky, almost like a man. 'She's menstrual, upset. And I'm her legal guardian an' I'm ready to go for the law right now.'

'No!' Danni's voice came from the depth of her body in a low growl. 'I kill myself. I *never* go with him!' And she pushed off the Orzel's hands to run and hide behind Tom: not behind the Eagle, nor big Frank Webb, but behind Tom.

'I s'pose the law's the law,' Dorota said, looking at Orzel. 'And we've got a publicans' licence to keep.'

Tom looked from one to another. There had been a time when he had to be silent for Danni's sake, at the docks. But now he had to help her by shouting out the awful truth. He twisted to the old man. 'There's other laws! What about the law against child abuse? Do you know the way he's been beating her, his belt hanging on the door?'

The woman in the doorway snorted and Harry shook his head and took a deep gulp from his glass. 'Oh, ain't it easy to say?' he said. 'To accuse. You give a kid guidelines, you set limits, when you're away a lot like me you have to, you have to know she's going to school – because it's me up in court if she ain't. An' it's natural they don't like it, what kid does? Rebellion, boy. But then they get in with a bad lot, all that ecstasy, an' snorting, an' you have to lay down the law…'

'Not!' Danni shouted. 'Not! That is lie!'

'…So they come up with some dirty little tale to get softies like this boy on their side.'

Danni came out from behind Tom. 'He is not softie!' she exploded. 'He is brave. Hero. He rescue me, save me, hide me, three days. He fight for me!' Danni was shaking her fist at the trucker. 'He is real man!'

For a moment Tom thought that was when Harry was going to make his move and go for her, he could see it in his eyes. He saw him look around at his sister, who nodded back at him.

'A father comes on a bit strong, OK, perhaps a bit too strong – and what do they do?' Harry asked. 'They up and off. Because it don't suit! But all ends up, I'm doing a father's duty, I'm telling you lot what the English law is an' I'm taking her home. An' what she's said is all in her head.'

'Not!' Danni shrieked.

'Why would she stab you, then?' Tom shouted at him. 'Kids run off but they don't try to kill! Why would she do that if you weren't evil?'

Now Tom thought Harry was going to come for him, never mind Danni. But the man's sudden movement was to open his jerkin top to the shirt, rip open the buttons and lift his vest. 'Where? Where did she stab me?' His chest was white and unmarked. 'Fantasy! Imagination!' He turned to Frank Webb.

But Danni cleared her throat, and her voice didn't lift from its low growl. 'Chest!' she said. 'Shut. This is not where I stab!' She looked up at Orzel now. 'I try to kill but he move, jump, so I stab where I can, different place. Top of leg. Ask why he limp!'

'Wrenched myself, that's all. My knee, getting out the lorry cab.'

'This is crazy talk!' growled the woman at the door.

The old airman had stood silent listening to all this and his expression hadn't changed, his eyes still burned into the room, his Polish ace's eyes on Harry. 'Crazy or not crazy, it is easy to know.' Now he stared at Harry with the determined look of a man about to give a burst of machine gun fire at an enemy. 'You say you wrench your knee. She says she stabs. So one is the truth, one is a lie. A stab is a stab; I can tell a stabbed groin from a hurt knee.' And almost under his breath as if the women mustn't hear he said, 'You come with me. Privately, we seal this, man and man…' And he took a step towards Harry.

'I'm not *stooping* to show anything to a *Pole*,'

Harry shouted. 'She's trash, this girl, gypsy Polski trash just like her mother – but she's mine, my daughter, and she's coming back with me!'

A glass suddenly crashed against the shelving above the bar. The sister had thrown it and all eyes went to it – except Harry's who straight off took his chance and grabbed Danni. In an instant he had her in the grip he'd had at the docks – and from his pocket had come a knife, a seaman's blade that he pointed at the room.

Danni screamed and kicked. Tom, Frank, Orzel, Dorota were on their toes – but no one moved within range of the weapon.

'Get the car!' Harry demanded – and his sister disappeared out of the door. 'This girl's coming home where she belongs. Father's rights.'

Danni bit him, kicked him, wriggled, pulled and pushed – but she couldn't get free. Tom's stomach was shot with adrenalin and his pulse was thumping. And he knew that whatever anyone else did or didn't do he was going to put up a fight. She might be Orzel's family – but she was his girlfriend.

'Yeah boy?' Harry had read his mind. 'Come on, then, if you fancy some...' And he backed towards the door.

'Leave it!' Frank said to Tom.

'There's other ways,' Dorota agreed.

'We will have justice,' Orzel called across the room. 'Poles have waited long for justice...'

'Bollocks!' said Harry.

From outside came the crunch of tyres on the gravel. Harry's knife hand went to the door handle. Tom knew if he got her to that car he'd have her – shut in tight at home. *His Danni!*

And without thinking, he went for the man. He didn't care! He could get cut, stabbed, he wasn't letting Harry out of that door with the girl he loved. He threw himself at the arm around Danni's throat, his eyes on the knife – to the agony of a sudden hard knee in the crotch that sent him sick and doubled to the floor. 'Aaah!'

'Leave it, boy!' Harry shouted – and yanked at the handle behind him.

Opening it to a big man in the doorway. George Welton. Tom's dad. Who saw Harry with the knife and Tom on the floor in pain – and who without a second's thought hit the trucker in the head with every ounce of strength a father could have.

'Told you I'd do the sorting!' he said to the pulp of the man's face, standing over Harry Smith till he pulled himself together enough to limp out of the door muttering threats through his swollen mouth – saying he'd be back – but he was finished.

At which, seeing him go, Danni suddenly pulled

herself away from Tom and threw herself down to slump at a table – where she hid her head in her arms and cried and cried and cried – years of long pent up tears: for her mother, for her own suffering, and for the childhood she had lost.

They left her to it, respected her need to grieve at last. Meanwhile, George Welton told them how he'd gone to Coltishall himself, not trusting the man, had come to where they'd directed. Drinks were quietly poured; Polish schnapps, the speciality of the house; while Dorota phoned social services – who came back to her with the news that although Danni's mother had married Harry, there was talk of some other wife somewhere, some other port.

'They say they're going to look into it, there's going to be fresh decisions made. But it don't look bad...'

The old air force ace came over to Tom where George Welton had a hand on his son's shoulder. At first he said nothing, just stood looking at him, nodding in some sort of acknowledgment, before he took Tom's hand and shook it firmly. 'You did these things she said? For her? For my family?'

Tom nodded. 'I s'pose like you in the war, there's no choice to make.'

'He did well, didn't he?' Tom's father said.

Orzel broke off and went to the mantelpiece, and from a trophy plaque at the side of his portrait he took something. He came back to Tom and pressed it into his hand, closing Tom's fingers over it. Slowly, Tom opened them to look at what he'd been given. It was a silver Polish Air Force eagle, the same as Danni's but full sized, the laurel wreath in the bird's beak a polished gold. The real thing. The old man took it again, and with the small wire hook on its chain he pinned it to Tom's chest, and he nodded.

'I think you could fly with me,' Orzel Mikawski said.

Tom had no words. He bowed his head in thanks.

'You know, I reckon he could,' George Welton said.

Tom had never felt so proud, so happy. He looked across the room at Danni who was coming up from her crying. He went over to her, sat down and held her hand – before touching his eagle's beak to hers. 'They kiss,' he said.

She looked him in the eyes; and in a quiet voice, just for him, she murmured, 'Tom. I love.'

And Tom Robinson's world was perfect.

I am indebted to the Imperial War Museum, the Royal Air Force Museum, Hendon and the Polish Air Force Association for their help with my research. My acknowledgment to them is at the end of the book so as not to give away aspects of the plot at the beginning!

The Polish 303 Squadron really existed although I have invented Orzel the Eagle and his family. 303's war record was remarkable. Its full name was No 303 Imieniem. T Koscinszko Fighter Squadron. Its famous squadron code was RF, changed to PD in 1945.

2,408 Polish airmen lost their lives flying with the RAF.

Other Black Apples
to get your teeth into...

BERNARD ASHLEY

1 84121 814 6 £4.99

Marsh End. Lonely, isolated and bleak, Sophia's mum loves it.

But for Sophia, the brooding skies hold no solace for her lost father, or her lost life in London. Nothing ever happens in this dead end place.

That is until Revenge House begins to reveal its murky secrets, and Sophia and her mum find themselves sucked into a brutal criminal underworld that will eventually threaten their lives.

BERNARD ASHLEY

1 86039 879 0 £4.99

When Kaninda survives a brutal attack on his village in East Africa, he joins the rebel army, where he's trained to carry weapons, and use them.

But aid workers take him to London where he fetches up in a comprehensive school. Clan and tribal conflicts are everywhere, and on the streets it's estate versus estate, urban tribe against urban tribe.

All Kaninda wants is to get back to his own war and take revenge on his enemies. But together with Laura Rose, the daughter of his new family, he is drawn into a dangerous local conflict that is spiralling out of control.

Shortlisted for the Carnegie Medal and the *Guardian* Children's Fiction Award

'So pacy that it is difficult to turn the pages fast enough.'
The School Librarian

'A gripping and compassionate tale.'
TES

BERNARD ASHLEY

1 86039 879 0   £4.99

Hard Stew always gets what he wants,
and he wants Davey's new bike.

But Hard Stew's not the only thing bothering
Davey, there's also the big family secret,
the one that everyone wants to keep from him.
A secret more frightening than a hundred Hard Stews.

The sort you've got to stare in the face.
If you've got the guts...

Shortlisted for the Sheffield Children's Book Award and the Angus Award

*'Bernard Ashley's great gift is to turn what seems
to be low-key realism into something much stronger
and more resonant.'*
Philip Pullman

MICHAEL COLEMAN

1 84362 183 5   £4.99

"You scared, Daniel?"

How many times has Tozer said that to me?
Hundreds.

But this time it's different. We're not in school.
He hasn't got me in a headlock, with one of
his powerful fists wrenching my arm up,
asking, "You scared, Weirdo?"

No. We're here, trapped underground together
with no way out.

**Shortlisted for the Carnegie Medal, the Lancashire
Children's Book Award and the Writers Guild Award**

'Tense and psychological.'
The Times

MICHAEL COLEMAN

1 84362 182 7   £4.99

It all started as a laugh, another of Motto's games. I only went along to help him out. I mean, that's what friends are for, isn't it?

Then we tangled with the Sun Crew.

Suddenly, I didn't have a friend. And the laughing had stopped.

Shortlisted for the Norfolk Libraries Children's Book Award

"Hard hitting, but subtle, with a clever twist at the end."
The Guardian

"A tense tight thriller."
Books for Keeps

ORCHARD BLACK APPLES

Little Soldier *Bernard Ashley*	1 86039 879 0	£4.99
Revenge House *Bernard Ashley*	1 84121 814 6	£4.99
Tiger Without Teeth *Bernard Ashley*	1 86039 879 0	£4.99
Going Straight *Michael Coleman*	1 84362 299 8	£4.99
Tag *Michael Coleman*	1 84362 182 7	£4.99
Weirdo's War *Michael Coleman*	1 84362 183 5	£4.99
Horowitz Horror *Anthony Horowitz*	1 84121 455 8	£4.99
More Horowitz Horror *Anthony Horowitz*	1 84121 607 0	£4.99
The Mighty Crashman *Jerry Spinelli*	1 84121 222 9	£4.99
Stargirl *Jerry Spinelli*	1 84121 926 6	£4.99
Get a Life *Jean Ure*	1 84121 831 6	£4.99

Orchard Black Apples are available from all good bookshops,
or can be ordered direct from the publisher:
Orchard Books, PO BOX 29, Douglas IM99 1BQ
Credit card orders please telephone 01624 836000
or fax 01624 837033 or visit our Internet site: www.wattspub.co.uk
or e-mail: bookshop@enterprise.net for details.

To order please quote title, author and ISBN
and your full name and address.
Cheques and postal orders should be made payable to 'Bookpost plc.'
Postage and packing is FREE within the UK
(overseas customers should add £1.00 per book).

Prices and availability are subject to change.